Writing the Critical Essay

RACISM

An OPPOSING VIEWPOINTS® Guide

Writing the Critical Essay

RACISM

An OPPOSING VIEWPOINTS® Guide

Other books in the Writing the Critical Essay series are:

Writing the Critical Essay

RACISM

An OPPOSING VIEWPOINTS® Guide

Lauri S. Friedman, *Book Editor*

Bonnie Szumski, *Publisher, Series Editor*
Helen Cothran, *Managing Editor*

OPPOSING
VIEWPOINTS®
SERIES

GREENHAVEN PRESS
An imprint of Thomson Gale, a part of The Thomson Corporation

THOMSON
GALE

Detroit • New York • San Francisco • San Diego • New Haven, Conn. • Waterville, Maine • London • Munich

LIBRARY OF CONGRESS CATALOGING-IN-PUBLICATION DATA

Racism / Lauri S. Friedman, book editor.
    p. cm. — (Writing the critical essay)
    Includes bibliographical references and index.
    ISBN 0-7377-3464-7 (lib. bdg. : alk. paper)
    1. Racism—United States. 2. United States—Race relations. 3. Essay—Authorship.
4. Rhetoric. 5. Critical thinking. I. Friedman, Lauri S. II. Series.
    E184.A1R326 2006
    305.800973—dc22
                                                                2005057099

Printed in the United States of America

CONTENTS

Examining the state of writing and how it is taught in the United States was the official purpose of the National Commission on Writing in America's Schools and Colleges. The commission, made up of teachers, school administrators, business leaders, and college and university presidents, released its first report in 2003. "Despite the best efforts of many educators," commissioners argued, "writing has not received the full attention it deserves." Among the findings of the commission was that most fourth-grade students spent less than three hours a week writing, that three-quarters of high school seniors never receive a writing assignment in their history or social studies classes, and that more than 50 percent of first-year students in college have problems writing error-free papers. The commission called for a "cultural sea change" that would increase the emphasis on writing for both elementary and secondary schools. These conclusions have made some educators realize that writing must be emphasized in the curriculum. As colleges are demanding an ever-higher level of writing proficiency from incoming students, schools must respond by making students more competent writers. In response to these concerns, the SAT, an influential standardized test used for college admissions, required an essay for the first time in 2005.

Books in the Writing the Critical Essay: An Opposing Viewpoints Guide series use the patented Opposing Viewpoints format to help students learn to organize ideas and arguments and to write essays using common critical writing techniques. Each book in the series focuses on a particular type of essay writing—including expository, persuasive, descriptive, and narrative—that students learn while being taught both the five-paragraph essay as well as longer pieces of writing that have an opinionated focus. These guides include everything necessary to help students research, outline, draft, edit, and ultimately write successful essays across the curriculum, including essays for the SAT.

Using Opposing Viewpoints

This series is inspired by and builds upon Greenhaven Press's acclaimed Opposing Viewpoints series. As in the parent series, each book in the Writing the Critical Essay series focuses on a timely and controversial social issue that provides lots of opportunities for creating thought-provoking essays. The first section of each volume begins with a brief introductory essay that provides context for the opposing viewpoints that follow. These articles are chosen for their accessibility and clearly stated views. The thesis of each article is made explicit in the article's title and is accentuated by its pairing with an opposing or alternative view. These essays are both models of persuasive writing techniques and valuable research material that students can mine to write their own informed essays. Guided reading and discussion questions help lead students to key ideas and writing techniques presented in the selections.

The second section of each book begins with a preface discussing the format of the essays and examining characteristics of the featured essay type. Model five-paragraph and longer essays then demonstrate that essay type. The essays are annotated so that key writing elements and techniques are pointed out to the student. Sequential, step-by-step exercises help students construct and refine thesis statements; organize material into outlines; analyze and try out writing techniques; write transitions, introductions, and conclusions; and incorporate quotations and other researched material. Ultimately, students construct their own compositions using the designated essay type.

The third section of each volume provides additional research material and writing prompts to help the student. Additional facts about the topic of the book serve as a convenient source of supporting material for essays. Other features help students go beyond the book for their research. Like other Greenhaven Press books, each book in the Writing the Critical Essay series includes bibliographic listings of relevant periodical articles, books, Web sites, and organizations to contact.

Writing the Critical Essay: An Opposing Viewpoints Guide will help students master essay techniques that can be used in any discipline.

Background to Controversy: Racism and War in the United States

As Japanese Americans learned during World War II, racism can be a particularly powerful force in times of war. After Japan attacked the United States in 1941 and drew it into the war against Japan and it allies, the U.S. government began to view its Japanese citizens as a threat to national security. Officials questioned their loyalty to the nation and feared they would commit acts of espionage or sabotage on behalf of Japan. As then–secretary of war Henry Stimson put it, "Their racial characteristics are such that we cannot understand or trust even the citizen Japanese."[1]

Therefore, in 1942 more than 110,000 Japanese Americans were rounded up and placed in internment camps scattered across the West Coast. Entire families were relocated and forced to live in the camps for the duration of the war. None of the internees was ever charged with a crime, and the homes and property they were forced to abandon were never returned to them. For Japanese Americans, fear and wartime conditions gave way to a serious wave of racism that until only recently was formally condemned by the government. An official apology was not issued until 1988, when President Ronald Reagan signed the Civil Liberties Act into law. The act stated the Japanese internment was "motivated largely by racial prejudice, wartime hysteria, and a failure of political leadership."[2]

Fear During War

More than sixty years after the Japanese were interned, America again finds itself grappling with a wave of racism born out of wartime and fear. This war began after

In this 1944 photo, a storeowner points proudly to a sign that makes clear his prejudice against Japanese Americans.

September 11, 2001, when nineteen Islamic fundamentalist terrorists hijacked planes and crashed them into American landmarks. The attacks launched the war on terrorism, which has taken the United States on military missions in Afghanistan, Iraq, and other Muslim nations such as Indonesia and the Philippines. These efforts, combined with frequent news about Islamic terrorists, have impacted the way in which some of America's Muslim and Arab citizens are treated and viewed.

Following the attacks, Arab and Muslim Americans experienced heightened violence, racism, and scrutiny. The Council on American-Islamic Relations (CAIR) reported 1,717 instances of harassment, violence, and other discriminatory acts against American Muslims in the first six months following 9/11. Groups such as CAIR also complain that Muslims of Middle Eastern origin have been singled out for inspection by the government. It is estimated that more than 200,000 Muslims have been investigated in the United States since September 11. Of these, a handful have been arrested for charges relating to terrorism. Similarly, the government's new policy of asking foreigners living in the United States to register with immigration officials has been selectively applied to immigrants from Egypt, Jordan, Kuwait, Saudi Arabia, Sudan, Libya, Iran, Iraq, and other predominantly Muslim countries. In addition, the Arab American Action Network claims the

Students in Berkeley, California, rally in support of Muslim and Arab Americans who fell victim to racist assaults in the wake of the September 11, 2001, terrorist attacks.

U.S. government has halved the number of acceptances of visitors' visa applications from Arab and Muslim countries. While many believe that these actions are justified considering the nature of the war on terror, others interpret them as unfair and racist. The network's director, Hatem Abudayyeh, has described these and other actions as "draconian measures and indiscriminate detentions and deportations [that] have destabilized and criminalized Arab communities across the United States."[3]

"Have Him Arrest Every Muslim"

Suspicion and even hatred of Arab and Muslim Americans has been publicly expressed by writers, politicians, reporters, and other people of prominence. In November 2001 Rep. C. Saxby Chambliss, a Republican from Georgia, suggested that Georgia law officers should "just turn [the sheriff] loose and have him arrest every Muslim that crosses the state line."[4] Chambliss chaired a House committee on terrorism and homeland security at the time of his comment.

In 2003 two women in New York protest against a program requiring immigrants from mostly Arab and Muslim countries to register with the government.

SPECIAL REGISTRATION TEARS FAMILIES APART!

END SPECIAL REGISTRATION NOW!

Echoing suspicion of Japanese Americans during World War II, the loyalty of Muslim Americans to the United States has also been quietly questioned. As columnist Srdja Trifkovic has put it, "Muslims are the only group that harbors a substantial segment of individuals who share key objectives with the terrorists. They are the immigrant group least likely to identify with America."[5]

Trifkovic has also suggested that, like the Japanese during World War II, Muslim Americans be registered and monitored by the government, and be barred from holding positions that require security clearance. A December 17, 2004, survey taken by Cornell University indicates that a sizable number of Americans agree with him. The poll found that 44 percent of Americans believe that government authorities should monitor Muslims living in America. Tactics include registering their whereabouts, monitoring their mosques, infiltrating their organizations, and keeping tabs on their fundraising activities. About 22 percent said the federal government should profile citizens as potential threats based solely on the fact that they are Muslim or have Middle Eastern heritage.

Dealing with Racism

Officially, the government has taken steps to protect Muslim and Arab Americans from unfair treatment and violence, indicating an important measure of support that the Japanese Americans never enjoyed. Four days after September 11, the House of Representatives passed a resolution formally condemning hate crimes against Arabs, Muslims, and South Asians. Echoing this sentiment, President Bush and other members of his administration have repeatedly told Americans that the war on terrorism should not be confused with a war on Islam, and called for Muslim Americans to be treated with tolerance and respect. Less than a week after the attacks Bush said:

> I've been told that some [Muslim Americans] fear to leave [their homes]; some don't want to go shopping

for their families; some don't want to go about their ordinary daily routines because . . . they're afraid they'll be intimidated. That should not and that will not stand in America.[6]

Arab and Muslim Americans are not the first immigrant group to experience racism that can flare up when the United States is at war with their homeland. Both during wartime and peacetime, racism and race continue to be a factor in personal relationships, professional endeavors, systematic procedures, and political initiatives. *Writing the Critical Essay: Racism* explores some of the ways in which racism is discussed in contemporary America. It also helps students formulate their own thoughts about racism. Through skill-building exercises and thoughtful discussion questions, students will formulate their own thoughts about racism and develop tools to craft their own essays on the subject.

Notes

1. Quoted in C. John Yu, "The Politician," February 3, 1997, www.oz.net.

2. Civil Liberties Act of 1988, 102 Stat. 94.

3. Quoted in Megan Harrington, "Arab and Muslim Immigrants Under Fire: Interview with Hatem Abudayyeh of the Arab American Action Network," *Dollars & Sense,* no. 248, July/August 2003.

4. Quoted in "Lawmaker Tries to Explain Remark; Rep. Chambliss, a Senate Hopeful, Commented on Muslims," *Washington Post,* November 21, 2001.

5. Srdja Trifkovic, "The Jihadist Fifth Column: The Cure," *Chronicles,* December 2004.

6. Remarks of President George W. Bush at the Islamic Center, September 17, 2001, www.usdoj.gov/crt/legal info/bushremarks.html.

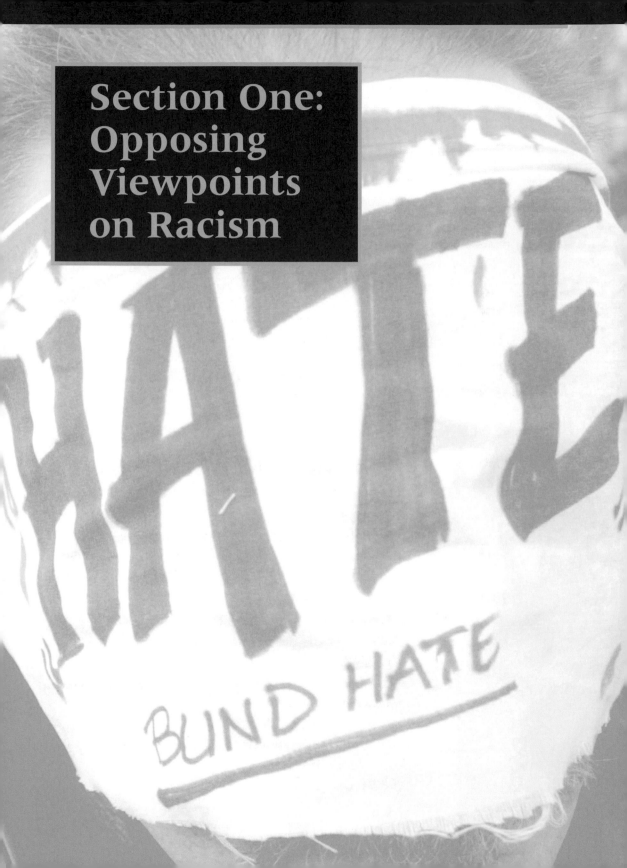

Section One:
Opposing
Viewpoints
on Racism

Racism Is a Serious Problem

Ziba Kashef

In the following viewpoint Ziba Kashef argues that minority groups continue to face racism on a daily basis in America. She cites a study undertaken by the Chicago Graduate School of Business and the Massachusetts Institute of Technology that found that employers tend to discriminate against job applicants if they have ethnic-sounding names. The study also found that people hired less qualified whites for jobs over better qualified blacks. The author hopes the next generation of Americans will put an end to the discrimination that was legally outlawed decades ago.

Kashef is a freelance writer based in San Francisco. Her articles have appeared in publications such as *ColorLines,* a quarterly journal that explores issues of race and culture.

Consider the following questions:

1. According to the author, how many more résumés might a man named Jamal Jones have to send out in order to get an interview, compared with a man named Brendan Baker?
2. Why was an Indian Canadian woman removed from an airplane after September 11, according to the author?
3. How did Stanford professor John Baugh experience racism while looking to buy a house, according to Kashef?

K
ofi? Mani? Sule? Bijan?

Choosing a name for my future son has turned out to be much more complicated than I thought when I started searching online for possibilities.

Reza? Omar? Darius? Malcolm?

Names Can Invite Racism

While I entertained the sound and significance of each potential moniker (Kofi is Twi for "born on Friday"—what if he's born on Tuesday?), I started to wonder about the consequences of giving him an obviously "ethnic" name. It would reflect his multiracial heritage (black, Iranian, Irish, Hungarian) and hopefully contribute to his sense of cultural pride. But the name would also likely be misspelled, mispronounced, and misunderstood in a country that is largely still ignorant and suspicious of otherness. . . .

So as I contemplate my son's name, I'm torn between the desire to emphasize his ethnicity and the desire to

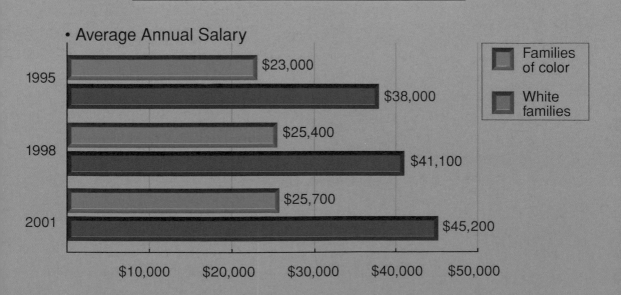

White Families Earn More Money than Families of Color per Year

• Average Annual Salary

Families of color

White families

1995
$23,000
$38,000

1998
$25,400
$41,100

2001
$25,700
$45,200

$10,000 $20,000 $30,000 $40,000 $50,000

Source: Ana M. Aizcorbe, Arthur B. Kennickell, and Kevin B. Moore, *Federal Reserve Bulletin*, January 2003.

minimize the potential for profiling and discrimination against him. While racial discrimination has been understood historically as a practice based on an individual's skin color, recent research is showing that it is also often based on a person's name or speech, with the same destructive effects.

Race Matters When Getting a Job

A name—and the racial group associated with it—can make the difference between getting a job interview and remaining unemployed, according to one recent study. Researchers at the University of Chicago Graduate School of Business and the Massachusetts Institute of Technology sent 5,000 fake resumes in response to a variety of ads in two major newspapers—the *Boston Globe* and the *Chicago Tribune*. Names on the resumes were selected to sound either distinctively Anglo (e.g., Brendan Baker) or African American (e.g., Jamal Jones). The study revealed that the fictitious job seekers with white names were 50 percent more likely to get calls for interviews. Those stats translate into the need for blacks to mail 15 resumes for every 10 resumes sent by whites in order to land one interview. Sadly, this pattern of affirmative action for white job hunters emerged even among federal contractors and firms that advertised themselves as "equal opportunity" employers.

Besides changing their names, there appears to be little black applicants can do to level the playing field. As part of the study, researchers created two sets of resumes—high quality and low quality—to reflect the actual pool of job seekers looking for work in fields ranging from sales, administrative support, clerical services, and customer services. But even having a higher quality resume

American Racism Is Institutionalized

The statistics . . . show that African Americans continue to lag behind whites in every possible category. Not only does this point to the depth of racial inequality in this society, but it clearly undermines the idea that racism is simply a matter of prejudice.

Keeanga-Yamahtta Taylor, "Racism in America Today," *International Socialist Review*, November/ December 2003.

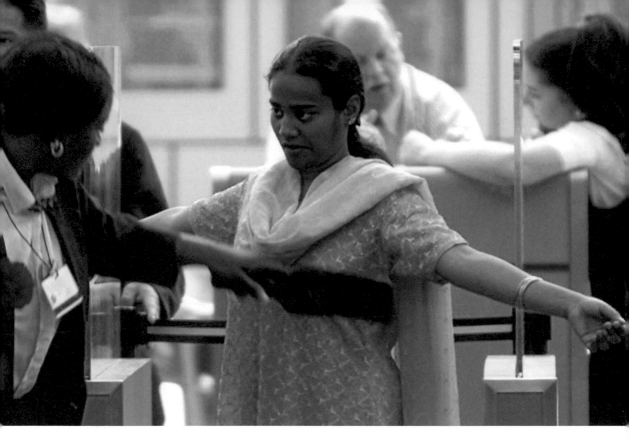

with such credentials as volunteer experience, computer skills, and special honors failed to improve the black applicants' chances of getting their foot in the door. "The payback that an African American applicant gets from building these skills is much lower than the payback a white applicant would get," the University of Chicago's associate professor Marianne Bertrand noted in a summary of the study.

A Muslim woman goes through airport security. After the September 11 attacks, screening procedures at airports were enhanced.

Discrimination of Travelers and Homebuyers

African and African American names aren't the only ones singled out for prejudice, of course, and the job sphere isn't the only realm in which such discrimination gets played out. In the American-Arab Anti-Discrimination Committee's (ADC) "Report on Hate Crimes and Discrimination Against Arab Americans: The Post–September 11 Backlash," the authors noted that among the dozens of instances of discrimination by airlines that occurred between September

Kirk. © 1998 by Kirk Anderson. Reproduced by permission.

2001 and October 2002, "the passenger's name or perceived ethnicity" alone was often sufficient cause for unpro-
voked removal from a flight. Discrimination often took place
whether or not the passenger was actually Arab or Muslim,
resulting in many South Asians and others falling victim to
the ignorance of the pilot or another passenger. According
to the ADC, one Indian Canadian woman was removed from
a plane because her last name was mispronounced as
"Attah" and therefore perceived as Middle Eastern. Other
passengers were prevented from traveling because their
names were similar to those on the FBI watch list. . . .

Names aren't the only potential cues to a person's
racial identity: speech may also reveal—or conceal—ethnicity. While searching for housing in the predominantly white neighborhood of Palo Alto, California, in the mid-
1990s, John Baugh made appointment after appointment
over the phone only to be turned away at the landlord's
door. "I was told that there was nothing available," says

the Stanford University professor of education and linguistics, who happens to be African American. It didn't take long for him to realize that prospective owners were mistaking his phone voice for that of a white person and inviting him to view apartments. When he showed up for the appointments, he was repeatedly told that there had been some misunderstanding. . . .

Hope for a Future of Acceptance

While blacks have long been the victims of such bias, Latinos, Asians, and Arab Americans—not to mention other vulnerable groups such as the elderly and disabled—are similarly profiled, experts note. Evidence of discrimination and laws to prevent it (such as the Fair Housing Act and Civil Rights Act) have failed to eradicate "talking while black" and other examples of linguistic racism. They remain largely invisible acts of bigotry—bloodless crimes that injure people of color while quietly reinforcing and perpetuating segregation and white supremacy. Perhaps by the time my future son is an adult, some 50 years after legal discrimination officially ended, he will grow up in a society where his ethnic name and heritage is truly accepted and not punished.

Analyze the essay:

1. Ziba Kashef frames her argument about racism by relaying a personal story about choosing her son's name. In your opinion, does casting the essay in the first person make the author's argument more believable or compelling? Why or why not?
2. The author tells the reader she is black and Iranian. Does knowing the author's ethnic background influence the way you interpret her essay? If so, in what way?

Racism Is Not a Serious Problem

Walter Williams

In the following essay Walter Williams argues that racism is not responsible for problems facing the black community. He argues that three problems facing blacks—low school performance, high prison population, and high illegitimacy rates (children born out of wedlock) can be blamed on the black community's refusal to take responsibility for itself. These problems will not be resolved, the author argues, until black leaders stop blaming racism.

Walter Williams is an economist. His articles have appeared in many conservative publications, including *Capitalism Magazine*, from which this viewpoint was taken.

Consider the following questions:

1. How does the author explain that black families were stronger during slavery than in modern times?
2. According to Williams, what is the high school graduation rate of black males?
3. What explanation does the author give for why Democrat politicians would want to perpetuate the idea of racism in America?

If you listened to the rhetoric of black politicians and civil rights leaders, dating back to the Reagan years, you would have been convinced that surely by now black Americans would be back on the plantation. According to them, President Reagan, and later Presidents Bush I and II, would turn back the clock on civil rights. They'd

Walter Williams, "Victimhood: Rhetoric or Reality," *Capitalism Magazine*, June 9, 2005. Copyright © 2005 by *Capitalism Magazine*™. All rights reserved. Reproduced by permission of Creators Syndicate, Inc.

appoint "new racists" dressed in three-piece suits to act through the courts and administrative agencies to reverse black civil rights and economic gains. We can now recognize this rhetoric as the political equivalent of the "rope-a-dope."

These fifth graders access the Internet from their classroom in Connecticut. Many argue that black and white students share the same educational opportunities.

As my colleague Tom Sowell pointed out in a recent column, "Liberals, Race and History," if the Democratic party's share of the black vote ever fell to even 70 percent, it's not likely that the Democrats would ever win the White House or Congress again. The strategy liberal Democrats have chosen, to prevent loss of the black vote, is to keep blacks paranoid and in a constant state of fear. But is it fear of racists, or being driven back to the plantation, that should be a top priority for blacks? Let's look at it.

Britt. © 1999 by Copley News Service. Reproduced by permission.

Blacks Play a Role in Their Problems

Only 30 to 40 percent of black males graduate from high school.

Many of those who do graduate emerge with reading and math skills of a white seventh- or eighth-grader. This is true in cities where a black is mayor, a black is superintendent of schools and the majority of principals and teachers are black. It's also true in cities where the per pupil education expenditures are among the highest in the nation.

Across the U.S., black males represent up to 70 percent of prison populations. Are they in prison for crimes against whites? To the contrary, their victims are primarily other blacks. Department of Justice statistics for 2001 show that in nearly 80 percent of violent crimes against blacks, both the victim and the perpetrator were the same race. In other words, it's not Reaganites, Bush supporters, right-wing ideologues or the Klan causing blacks to live in fear of their lives and property and making their neighborhoods economic wastelands.

What about the decline of the black family? In 1960, only 28 percent of black females between the ages of 15 and 44 were never married.

Today, it's 56 percent. In 1940, the illegitimacy rate among blacks was 19 percent, in 1960, 22 percent, and today, it's 70 percent. Some argue that the state of the black family is the result of the legacy of slavery, discrimination and poverty. That has to be nonsense. A study of 1880 family structure in Philadelphia shows that three-quarters of black families were nuclear families, comprised of two parents and children. In New York City in 1925, 85 percent of kin-related black households had two parents. In fact, according to Herbert Gutman in "The Black Family in Slavery and Freedom: 1750–1925," "Five in six children under the age of 6 lived with both parents." Therefore, if one argues that what we see today is a result of a legacy of slavery, discrimination and poverty, what's the explanation for stronger black families at a time much closer to slavery—a time of much greater discrimination and of much greater poverty? I think that a good part of the answer is there were no welfare and Great Society programs.[1]

> ## Racism Is Not Black America's Biggest Problem
>
> Racism is no longer the major problem facing American blacks. . . . What is? A list of likely culprits would surely include the collapse of the black family, the failure of the public schools and black-on-black crime.
>
> Linda Chavez, "NAACP Time Warp," *Washington Times*, July 19, 2003.

Stop Preaching Victimhood

Since black politicians and the civil rights establishment preach victimhood to blacks, I'd prefer that they be more explicit when they appear in public fora. Were they to be

---

1. The author is referring to public programs that assist the poor. He believes such programs remove people's incentives to better themselves.

so, saying racists are responsible for black illegitimacy, blacks preying on other blacks and black family breakdown, their victimhood message would be revealed as idiotic. But being so explicit is not as far-fetched as one might think. In a campaign speech before a predominantly black audience, in reference to so many blacks in prison, presidential candidate John Kerry said, "That's unacceptable, but it's not their fault."

Analyze the essay:

1. The author of this viewpoint, Walter Williams, is black. Does knowing this change the way in which you receive his arguments? If so, in what way?

2. In the previous essay, author Ziba Kashef argues that racism is a serious problem facing minorities in America. In this essay, Williams rejects the idea that racism is holding minorities back. After reading both essays, which viewpoint do you agree with? What was most convincing about the article?

Racial Profiling Is Necessary

Philip Jenkins

In the following viewpoint Philip Jenkins uses a creative narrative to argue that racial profiling can prevent terrorism and other crime. He pretends that he has obtained an article written in an alternate reality, one in which the terrorist attacks of September 11, 2001, never occurred. In this alternate reality, the authorities used racial profiling to apprehend the hijackers before they were able to strike. Jenkins writes how the use of racial profiling turned into a scandal and that America lamented that such harmless men were subjected to the practice. Through this narrative device, Jenkins shows his belief that it is important to use racial profiling to catch terrorists even if it is not a politically correct practice.

Jenkins is the author of *Images of Terror: What We Can and Can't Know About Terrorism*.

Consider the following questions:

1. In the author's alternate reality, what was the scandal known as "Septembergate"?
2. Why do you think in his alternate reality the author describes Mohammad Atta as "a gentle, pious soul"?
3. Jenkins concludes his fictional article by saying "America holds no values higher than protecting ethnic minorities against an out-of-control justice system." Do you think he really means this?

Some people argue racial profiling could have prevented the five terrorists who boarded American Airlines Flight 11 (inset) from crashing the plane into the North Tower of the World Trade Center (pictured).

L et me apologize. A massive technical glitch, involving distortions of the fourth dimension, has prevented me from researching the column I intended to write about ethnic and racial profiling. The column would have pointed out that many people who complain about profiling fail to define just what the term means. They confuse blatant examples of crude racial discrimination—police stopping people solely on the basis of "Driving While Black"—with the intelligent and selective use of race and ethnicity as crucial factors in criminal investigation. . . .

As I said, however, I am unable to write that column. What happened was this: In looking for background on profiling, I ordered a copy of the latest *Almanac of American Politics*. Because of a mix-up at *Amazon.com*, though, I was accidentally sent a copy from an alternate world, where the current of reality diverged from our own. Just out of curiosity, anyway, I now present the discussion that the alternative *Almanac* offers on the profiling issue.

If the Hijackers Had Been Caught

"Now that ethnic profiling has become the decisive political theme it has, it is difficult to recall what a fringe issue this was before the epoch-making events of September 2001. Though the Septembergate story has been told often enough, we must still be startled at the astonishingly bigoted behavior of the administration and the federal justice agencies. Their official rationale was this: The FBI and CIA had come to believe that Islamic terrorists were planning to use aircraft in a massive terrorist attack on U.S. soil; that some of their militants were already in the United States; and that they had received training in flying large airliners. Putting two and two together, federal agencies decided that Middle Eastern terrorists planned to crash several hijacked airliners into major buildings, including the World Trade Center, the Capitol, and the Pentagon. Responding to this far-fetched notion, the FBI searched the records of U.S. flight schools to find Arab or Middle Eastern men who had received training in the previous two or three years and placed these individuals under surveillance. Airports were given strict instructions to search anyone on the official watch-list and to look especially for edged weapons. On September 10, 2001, Attorney General John Ashcroft announced the arrest of 20 Arab men, chiefly from Saudi Arabia and Yemen.

> ## Terrorists Can Be Profiled
>
> Islamic terrorists will necessarily be Muslims, and probably from the Arab world. Not to profile for those characteristics is simply to ignore the nature of today's terrorism.
>
> Richard Lowry, "Profiles in Cowardice," *National Review*, January 28, 2002.

"Initially, the media paid polite attention to the news, but, over the following weeks, interest gave way to derision. On the comedy programs [Jay] Leno and [David] Letterman ridiculed the idea of these 'losers'—who could not even afford real weapons—trying to hijack an airliner, let alone knowing what to do with it once they had done so. *Saturday Night Live* reconstructed the event in an hilarious sketch, with shrieking turbaned Arabs running into cockpits, armed with tiny plastic scissors. Hundreds of

Lester. © 2004 by Mike Lester. All rights reserved. Reproduced by permission.

thousands signed a humorous e-mail petition circulated nationwide, declaring support for anyone prepared to blow up the Pentagon. And, as all the experts made clear, even if an airliner succeeded in approaching the World Trade Center, an impact would have had no effect whatever on the building's structural soundness.

The "September 10" Scandal

"But humor soon turned to fury, as financial and corporate scandals erupted and the public came to suspect the cynical agenda motivating the persecution of the hapless Arab suspects. . . . The perception that charges had been trumped-up was confirmed when millions watched [CNN's] Larry King's interview with [9/11 hijacker] Mohammed Atta, following his release on bail. At first hand, the audience saw that such a gentle, pious soul could never be a terrorist.

"Meanwhile, congressional investigators focused on the blatant and unapologetic uses of ethnic profiling by the FBI and CIA. In blatantly discriminatory terms, agents were told to watch for 'Arab and Middle Eastern' men attending flight schools; they were told to exercise surveillance over 'Arabs' boarding planes in groups and even to prevent them from boarding. Some harrowing documents told agents to seek out 'radical Muslim' extremists, confirming charges of religious bigotry. When former President Clinton spoke of the naked discrimination displayed in the arrest of the September 10 suspects, he remarked that 'Freedom itself was attacked that morning, and freedom will be defended.' Finding so many smoking guns, liberal and left-wing campaigns succeeded in forcing the resignations of [former attorney general] John Ashcroft and CIA Director George Tenet. Activists also used the September 10 scandal to raise public consciousness of bias in the justice system, and sweeping legislation prohibited all use of racial or ethnic data in criminal investigation. . . .

"By bringing racial discrimination to the foreground of American political debate, September 10 had a truly incalculable effect on the nation's public life. It brought home to us once and for all that America holds no values higher than protecting ethnic minorities against an out-of-control justice system."

Analyze the essay:

1. Jenkins conjures up the story about how he obtained an article from another dimension in order to argue that racial profiling is justified. What is your opinion of this writing technique? Identify a couple of ways it differs from a traditional essay. Articulate which style you prefer, and why.

2. In his depiction of an alternate reality, Jenkins intentionally ridicules events that actually happened. For example, he makes fun of the idea that planes could be hijacked with anything but "real weapons." He also invents experts that say that a plane crash would have no effect on the World Trade Center. Why do you think he makes up these kinds of details? What do you think he is getting at?

Racial Profiling Is Unnecessary

David Harris

In the following essay David Harris argues that racial pro-filing is ineffective and unnecessary. He points out that focusing on race distracts law enforcement officials from searching for suspicious behavior, which is more likely to indicate terrorist activity. He also argues that profiling vio-lates the rights of Arab and Muslim Americans, who could help officials collect intelligence. Finally, Harris argues that focusing on a particular racial profile will be useless should the terrorists decide to send someone outside of the pro-file, such as a woman, or anyone other than a Middle Eastern man. He concludes that using stereotypes to fight terror hurts authorities' chances of catching terrorists.

Harris is a professor of law at the University of Toledo College of Law and the author of *Profiles in Injustice: Why Racial Profiling Cannot Work*.

Consider the following questions:

1. According to the author, what might be suspi-cious about a one-way ticket bought with cash?
2. What did the law enforcement community *not* do in the wake of the Oklahoma City Bombings?
3. In the author's opinion, what will be the "per-verse" effect of racial profiling Middle Easterners?

September 11 [2001] dramatically recast the issue of racial profiling. Suddenly, racial profiling was not a discred-ited law enforcement tactic that alienated and injured cit-izens while it did little to combat crime and drugs; instead,

David Harris, "Flying While Arab: Lessons from the Racial Profiling Controversy," *Civil Rights Journal*, Winter 2002. Copyright © 2002 by the U.S. Commission on Civil Rights. Reproduced by permission.

American Attitudes on Racial Profiling

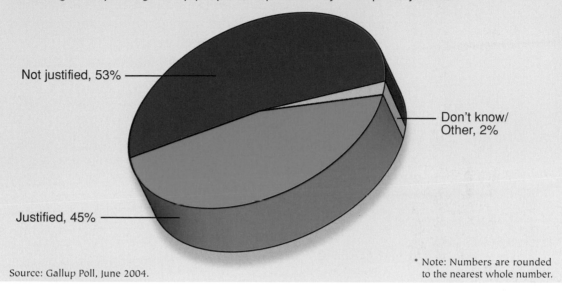

A Gallup poll conducted in June 2004 asked Americans the following question: Is using racial profiling to stop people at airport security checkpoints justified?

Not justified, 53%

Don't know/ Other, 2%

Justified, 45%

Source: Gallup Poll, June 2004.

* Note: Numbers are rounded to the nearest whole number.

it became a vital tool to assure national security, especially in airports. The public discussion regarding the targets of profiling changed too—from African Americans, Latinos, and other minorities suspected of domestic crime, especially drug crime, to Arab Americans, Muslims, and others of Middle Eastern origin, who looked like the suicidal hijackers of September 11. In some respects, this was not hard to understand. The September 11 attacks had caused catastrophic damage and loss of life among innocent civilians; people were shocked, stunned, and afraid. And they knew that all of the hijackers were Arab or Middle Eastern men carrying out the deadly threats of Osama bin Laden's al Qaeda terrorist network based in the Middle East, which of course claims Islam as its justification for the attacks and many others around the world. Therefore, many said that it just makes sense to profile people who looked Arab, Muslim, or Middle Eastern. After all, "they" were the ones who'd carried out the attacks and continued to threaten us; ignoring these facts amounted to some kind of political correctness run amok in a time of great danger. . . .

But . . . we should learn from what we now know were the grand mistakes of profiling in the last 10 years. If we do that, we will see that using Arab or Muslim background or appearance to profile for potential terrorists will almost certainly fail—even as it damages our enforcement efforts and our capacity to collect intelligence. . . .

Profiling Drains Enforcement Efforts

Even if the suicide hijackers of September 11 shared a particular ethnic appearance or background, subjecting all Middle Easterners to intrusive questioning, stops, or searches will have a perverse and unexpected effect: it will spread our enforcement and detection efforts over a huge pool of people who police would not otherwise think worthy of attention. The vast majority of people who look like Mohammed Atta and the other hijackers will never have anything to do with any kind of ethnic or religious extremism. Yet a profile that includes race, ethnicity, or religion may well include them, drawing them into the universe of people who law enforcement will stop, question, and search. Almost all of them will be people who would not otherwise have attracted police attention, because no other aspect of their behavior would have drawn scrutiny. Profiling will thus drain enforcement efforts and resources away from more worthy investigative efforts and tactics that focus on the close observation of behavior— like the buying of expensive one-way tickets with cash just a short time before takeoff, as some of the World Trade Center hijackers did. . . .

Behavior Tells More than Race

Second, and perhaps more important, focusing on race and ethnicity keeps police attention on a set of surface details that tells us very little and draws officers' attention away from what is much more important and concrete: behavior. The two most important tools law enforcement agents have in preventing crime and catching criminals are observation of behavior and intelligence. As any experienced police officer knows, what's important in understanding who's up to no good is not what people look like, but what they do. Investigating people who "look suspicious" will often lead officers down the wrong path; the key to success is to observe behavior. Anyone who simply looks different may seem strange or suspicious to the untrained eye; the veteran law enforcement officer knows that suspicious behavior is what really should attract attention and investigation. Thus focusing on those who "look suspicious" will necessarily take police attention away from those who act suspicious. . . .

Timothy McVeigh (inset) bombed the Murrah Federal Building in Oklahoma City in 1995. As a white war veteran, McVeigh would not have come under suspicion using racial profiling.

Kirk. © 2001 by Kirk Anderson. Reproduced by permission.

Third, if observation of suspicious behavior is one of law enforcement's two important tools, using profiles of Arabs, Muslims, and other Middle Easterners can damage our capacity to make use of the other tool: the gathering, analysis, and use of intelligence. There is nothing exotic about intelligence; it simply means information that can be useful in crime fighting. If we are concerned about terrorists of Middle Eastern origin, among the most fertile places from which to gather intelligence will be the Arab American and Muslim communities. If we adopt a security policy that stigmatizes every member of these groups in airports and other public places with intrusive stops, questioning, and searches, we will alienate them from the enforcement efforts at precisely the time we need them most. And the larger the population we subject to this treatment, the greater the total amount of damage we inflict on law-abiding persons.

Don't Assume All Terrorists Will Look the Same

And of course the profiling of Arabs and Muslims assumes that we need worry about only one type of terrorist. We must not forget that, prior to the attacks on September 11, the most deadly terrorist attack on American soil [the 1995 Oklahoma City Bombing] was carried out not by Middle

Easterners with Arabic names and accents, but by two very average American white men: Timothy McVeigh, a U.S. Army veteran from upstate New York, and Terry Nichols, a farmer from Michigan. Yet we were smart enough in the wake of McVeigh and Nichols' crime not to call for a profile emphasizing the fact that the perpetrators were white males. The unhappy truth is that we just don't know what the next group of terrorists might look like. . . .

With enemies of such craftiness and determination, it seems extremely unlikely that they will use people for their next attack who look like exactly what we are looking for. Rather, they will shift to light-skinned people who look less like Arabs or Middle Easterners, without Arabic names, or to people who are not Middle Easterners at all, such as individuals from African nations or the Philippines. (In both places, there are significant numbers of Muslims, a small but significant number of whom have been radicalized.) This, of course, will put us back where we started, and racial or ethnic appearance will become a longest-of-long-shot, almost certainly an ineffective predictor at best, and a damaging distracting factor at worst.

Analyze the essay:

1. In this viewpoint David Harris argues that racial profiling is unnecessary and ineffective. In the previous viewpoint Philip Jenkins argues that racial profiling could have prevented the September 11 attacks. After reading both viewpoints, which author do you agree with? Was there a particular piece of evidence or writing technique that swayed you? Explain.
2. In arguing against the practice of racial profiling, Harris mentions Timothy McVeigh and Terry Nichols. Why does he do this? How does this strengthen his argument that racial profiling is ineffective?

My Encounters with Racism

Ted Gup

In the following essay Ted Gup recounts his experience with an anti-Semitic restaurant owner to argue that free speech should be allowed, even if it is offensive. He describes the hateful images that decorate the walls of the restaurant and discusses the impact racism has had on his life, including his South Korean sons' painful experiences with racism at school. While offended and hurt by the cruelty of racists, Gup believes that such ideas should be out in the open so that they can be challenged.

Gup is a professor of journalism at Case Western Reserve University in Cleveland, Ohio.

Consider the following questions:

1. What does the word *antiseptic* mean in the context of the essay?
2. Describe three offensive items found at Grandpa's Kitchen.
3. What does the author think his visit with Brahim "Abe" Ayad might have accomplished?

I would like to have lunch at Grandpa's Kitchen, a convenience store and deli on East 55th and Chester. But despite its warm and fuzzy name, I fear that I would not be entirely welcome there. I say this because of the huge

Jewish men inspect headstones desecrated by French neo-Nazis in 2004.

mural on the side of the building that depicts Jews as monkeys wearing yarmulkes. [1]

The owner, a Mr. Brahim "Abe" Ayad, has made it pretty clear that he is none too fond of people of my faith. He has his reasons, many of them involving his father, a Palestinian who he says was driven from his land to make way for the state of Israel. Today, Grandpa's Kitchen is a kind of local landmark, a testament to unmuzzled anti-Semitism. But the fact that this animosity has been allowed to fester publicly is one that I, the grandson of a rabbi, applaud without reservation. . . .

1. Yarmulkes are caps worn by observant Jews.

Q: What's black and white and Stupid all over?

RACISM

Ramirez. © 1995 by Copley News Service. Reproduced by permission.

Words Can Be Ugly

I understand the emotional appeal of speech code[2] and I well know how noxious and hurtful words can be. As a Jew growing up in Ohio in the 1950s, I was branded a "shylock" and a "kike." I was threatened and, on occasion, beaten. In junior high, two classmates stabbed me with a pencil, and four decades later, two graphite points are still plainly visible in my left hand. That helped clarify for me the difference between speech and action, or the "sticks and stones" rule of the playground. Today my sons, adopted from South Korea, also know that words can be ugly. I listen in pained silence as they tell me of classmates who taunt them by pinching the corners of their own eyes or call them "chinks." Over a soda, I tell my son who gets off the yellow school bus with a black eye that I understand, even if I can't explain what fuels his tormenters.

But as a journalist and as an American, I feel a curious, almost perverse, sense of pride that Grandpa's Kitchen, with its notorious mural, could find a secure place

2. that is, laws that would make hate speech illegal

in this city of immigrants and minorities. Beyond that, I have a feeling that Abe (as I have begun to think of him) may have something to teach me and that I owe him—no, I owe myself—a visit. . . .

Offensive Images and Accusations

The first thing I see as I pull up to the deli is the mural, a pastiche of offensive images and accusations. One depicts a Jewish conspiracy in control of American network television. Another shows Jesus Christ in agony on the cross. Just inside the door, a news article is tacked to the wall: "Tel Aviv Mayor Seeks Help in Cleveland." Above it is written "Proof Implicating Jews." Am I not now in hostile territory? . . .

French Jews protest a wave of anti-Semitic attacks on Jewish schools, cemeteries, and synagogues in France in 2002.

I had expected someone consumed with hate and at first he confirms my stereotype. He hands me a book entitled "The Ugly Truth About the ADL [Anti-Defamation League[3]]." He calls 9/11 a Jewish conspiracy and produces a poster depicting Israeli leaders astride missiles labeled "Nuke" and "Chemical." Their target is spelled out: "Islam World or Bust." . . .

What is it, I ask him, that he hopes to accomplish with his attacks on Jews? "It should be perceived as a plea for help," he says. "I'm not going to hurt anybody. That is not even an option." He adds, "I just want to vent my frustrations and my disappointments. How else could I get their attention?" And then there is his quixotic effort to win back lands he says were his father's and are his rightful inheritance, land on which, he says, there are now Jewish settlements and factories. "ALL I WANT IS MY LAND" is painted on the mural. "I just want justice. I can't ask for revenge—that's God's. I'm just trying to break the cycle of hate that's been consuming us."

But how can he expect to promote understanding while using words of hate? How misguided, I think. . . .

My Own Best Defense

The landscape of my youth had no such murals of intolerance. Instead, prejudice was hidden behind disingenuous smiles and behind the manicured hedges of off-limits country clubs and the ivied walls of universities with secret quotas. As a boy in Canton, Ohio, I remember my family fantasized about living beside a lake on the edge of town, but we knew it was closed to "our kind." The word that was

---

3. a Jewish organization that fights anti-Semitism

Couples lunch at an exclusive country club in 1955. Many such country clubs barred Jews from becoming members.

used, if it was uttered at all, was "restricted." How anti-septic. . . .

Speech codes threaten to take us back to the old days when prejudice was vented only in whispers between like minds. My own history has convinced me that a silenced bigot can do far more mischief than one who airs his hatred publicly. . . .

That's why I defend Abe's right to express his hostilities. I see it as my own best defense.

Don't get me wrong. The murals make me cringe, but I much prefer that his feelings be out in the open. They tell me where I stand with Abe. They also invite the possibility, however slim, that we might find some sliver of common ground, that confrontation could lead to conciliation. . . .

I wince when I hear raw ethnic, racial and sexual slurs. But even worse is the notion that people who think that way could move about among us, unknown and unchallenged. "You can't cure it if you can't hear it," my mother says. She's right. Bigotry is an affliction not of the mouth but of the mind. . . .

I have no illusion that my visit with Abe changed his mind about Jews or put out years of smoldering resentment, but it did open a dialogue and, humble as that may be, it is a start.

Analyze the essay:

1. In this essay Gup uses his personal encounters with racism to express his belief that no matter how offensive, a person's right to free speech should never be violated. Do you agree with him? What do you think the use of first-person narrative lends to the essay?

2. Gup describes several instances in his life where he has encountered racism. Examine one of these passages and note the words and phrases that you think make the anecdotes powerful or compelling.

My Life as a Former White Supremacist

Kevin J. Marinelli

The following essay was written by former white supremacist Kevin J. Marinelli, who was convicted of murder in
February 1997 and sentenced to death. He uses personal
anecdotes and narrative to describe his experiences in the
New Nation Skinheads. He explains how he was drawn
into the group, what fueled his racism, and how he came
to question the movement's ideas. Ultimately, Marinelli
came to see racism as hypocritical and regrets that his life
was ruined by what he calls the lie of white supremacy.

Marinelli currently sits on death row in Pennsylvania.

Consider the following questions:

1. What did the author learn from reading Adolf
   Hitler's book, *Mein Kampf*?
2. Who is Rob Stoud?
3. According to Marinelli, what happened on
   December 23, 1993?

After being honorably discharged from the Army in
1992 because my recruiter screwed up my enlistment
papers, I lost my Pell Grant after only a semester of college. I was dejected, disenchanted, and had pretty much
given up on myself. Then I ran into Rob Stoud, founder of
the "New Nation Skinheads" (NNS) and an old acquain-
tance of mine, during a confrontation with the skins. While
my friend Jerry Miller was trying to join the group, I was
exposed to their ideology, parties and music. I was already

Kevin J. Marinelli, "Boneheads from the Inside Out: An Account from Death Row,"
Turning the Tide, March/April 2005. Copyright © 2005 by Kevin J. Marinelli. Reproduced
by permission.

into heavy metal, boozing and violence, so I didn't need any conversion there. I guess I was appealing to them because I look like a Celt and I'm ex-military.

The Center of My Existence

In January 1993, I became convinced the tough breaks in my life were part of an elaborate, if improbable, Jewish conspiracy. "It wasn't your fault!" I heard, and it was what I wanted to hear. I was given an enemy, and a cause or goal to strive for. This gave meaning and purpose to my life, along with camaraderie and acceptance. I quickly submerged myself in skinhead/racist literature, and made "the Cause" the center of my existence.

When I got forced out of my job at Pizza Hut for being a skinhead, it only made me more determined and radical. I even got my brother Mark involved. I saw us as soldiers in a race war. . . .

Bennett. © by King Features Syndicate. Reproduced by permission.

Violence and Harassment

On June 6, 1993, I initiated three new guys into the group—only Stoud and I ever did that, everybody else was voted in. Afterward, we went out for drinks. Two of the new skins got their heads smacked together by someone, and did nothing about it. I ended up repeatedly stabbing and slashing the guy who did it. . . .

In November [1993], we went to hassle what we thought was supposed to be a gay rally. The KKK was supposed to be there, too. We were so disorganized, we didn't know the event was actually "Hands Across Bloomsburg," in honor of a Black family that died when a burning cross fell on their house. All the racist skins did was stand around shouting childish comments. One guy talked to the media—which was supposedly controlled by the Jews, so why talk to them? . . . I was belligerent, yelling "Sieg Heil!" [1] during the "moment of silence.". . .

The Ku Klux Klan, seen here at a cross-burning rally in Georgia, is one of the best-known white supremacist groups in the United States.

1. "Sieg Heil" means "Hail Victory" in German. It was frequently shouted at Nazi rallies and speeches when Adolf Hitler ruled Germany.

Rethinking White Supremacy

[After several disagreements with the skins,] I decided to get an education from another source. I went to the library, and read "Mein Kampf" [by Adolf Hitler] and "The Rise and Fall of the Third Reich," and realized the situation was even worse than I had previously thought. I had always thought it was strange that Brian was Cherokee Indian and a skinhead. According to Hitler, he'd be dead! Me, too—I'm part Indian and part Polish. Hearing what the Nazis had done to the Poles [during World War II] really set me on fire. Not to mention that none of us Nazis should be drinking alcohol, sexually promiscuous, uneducated and unemployed. I was the only one with even a diploma. And these skins were always talking trash about Blacks, saying how they sell drugs—and they were the ones buying them! I'd had it, I was done with them for good.

Of course this didn't go over real well with the NNS, especially because I didn't pull any punches about what losers I thought they were. "You're a bunch of uneducated drunks and I don't want anything to do with you." It was a bitter pill for them, but what were they going to do? I had more courage in my pinkie than the lot of them.

After 10 months with the skins, I had destroyed my life and brought grief on my family, spent four months in jail with the charges still pending, and screwed up my chances of getting back into the Army. I was having trouble dropping my racist attitudes, too. It was like an addict being drawn to the very thing he knows and admits is harmful to him. I still had a "white pride" thing I was nursing. . . .

> ## White Supremacy on the Rise
>
> White supremacists have taken a long march from the margins to the mainstream, like a guerilla army slowly encircling the cities. After 20 years of torchlight rallies, preaching, radio broadcasts and grass-roots organizing, they have built a distinctive constituency and counterculture institutions.
>
> Leonard Zeskind, "This Killer Didn't Just Blindly Hate: He Hated with a Vision," *Los Angeles Times*, July 7, 1999.

The Abandoned Island of Death Row

On December 23 [1993], I was on my way out [of the group] when three nazi-skins [found me]. I guess this was payback. One guy held me down as another repeatedly kicked me in the face. Unfortunately for them, I had been on my way to return a 3-pound sledgehammer to a friend. I managed to get my hands on it, and smashed one in the head. He loosened his grip and I smashed the knee of the dude who was kicking me. Within seconds they scampered off and I was left with a broken nose, my blood on the floor and their blood all over the walls. . . .

Things were quiet until May 1994, when I got arrested for robbery-murder on a white guy [that was committed on April 26, 1994] and ten other cases totaling 56 charges. . . .

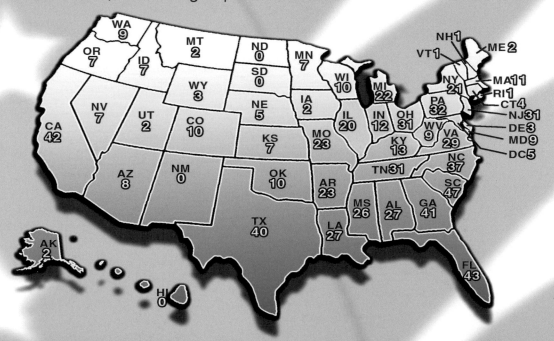

Hate Groups in the United States

As of 2004, 762 hate groups were active in the United States.

WA 9 · OR 7 · ID 7 · MT 2 · ND 0 · SD 0 · MN 7 · WI 10 · MI 22 · NH 1 · VT 1 · ME 2 · NY 21 · MA 11 · RI 1 · CT 4 · NV 7 · UT 2 · WY 3 · NE 5 · IA 2 · IL 20 · IN 12 · OH 31 · PA 32 · NJ 31 · DE 3 · CA 42 · CO 10 · KS 7 · MO 23 · KY 13 · WV 9 · VA 29 · MD 9 · DC 5 · AZ 8 · NM 0 · OK 10 · AR 23 · TN 31 · NC 37 · SC 47 · TX 40 · LA 27 · MS 26 · AL 27 · GA 41 · AK 2 · HI 0 · FL 43

Source: Tolerance.org, 2005. www.tolerance.org.

I found myself isolated and stuck between a rock and hard place. The DA [district attorney] was using innuendoes of my previous racist affiliations to prejudice the jury against me, and the racist skinheads were testifying against me because I wasn't one of them any longer. Either way, I was going to be smashed on the rocks; I ended up shipwrecked on the abandoned island of Death Row, which is where I now reside. Here I have sat for a little over a decade, facing execution. A direct line can be drawn back from here to January 1993, when I bought the lie of white supremacy.

Analyze the essay:

1. Marinelli fully regrets his racist past while on death row for his crimes. Do you think his story could convince other white supremacists to reject their beliefs? Why or why not?
2. The author describes at least three factors that influenced his decision to join the New Nation Skinheads. What are these factors? In your opinion, which of these had the greatest effect on him? Explain.

Section Two:
Model Essays
and Writing
Exercises

The Five-Paragraph Essay

An essay is a short piece of writing that discusses or analyzes one topic. The five-paragraph essay is a form commonly used in school assignments and tests. Every five-paragraph essay begins with an introduction, ends with a conclusion, and features three supporting paragraphs in the middle.

The Thesis Statement. The introduction includes the essay's thesis statement. The thesis statement presents the argument or point the author is trying to make about the topic. The essays in this book all have different thesis statements because they are making different arguments about racism.

The thesis statement should be a clear statement that tells the reader what the essay will be about. A focused thesis statement helps determine what will be in the essay; the subsequent paragraphs are spent developing and supporting its argument.

The Introduction. In addition to presenting the thesis statement, a well-written introductory paragraph captures the attention of the reader and explains why the topic being explored is important. It may provide the reader with background information on the subject matter or feature an anecdote that illustrates a point relevant to the topic. It could also present startling information that clarifies the point of the essay or present a contradictory position that the essay will refute.

The Supporting Paragraphs. The introduction is followed by three (or more) supporting paragraphs. These are the main body of the essay. Each paragraph presents and develops a subtopic that supports the essay's thesis statement. Each subtopic is then supported with its own facts, details, and examples. The writer can use various kinds of supporting material and details to back up the topic of each supporting paragraph. These may include statistics, quotations from people with special knowledge or expertise, historic facts, and anecdotes. A rule of writing is that specific and concrete examples are more convincing than vague, general, or unsupported assertions. When writing narrative essays, subtopics may consist of new pieces of the story being told.

The Conclusion. The conclusion is the paragraph that closes the essay. Its function is to summarize or reiterate the main idea of the essay. It may recall an idea from the introduction or briefly examine the larger implications of the thesis. Because the conclusion is also the last chance a writer has to make an impression on the reader, it is important that it not simply repeat what has been presented elsewhere in the essay but close it in a clear, final, and memorable way.

Although the order of the essay's component paragraphs is important, they do not have to be written in that order. Some writers like to decide on a thesis and write the introductory paragraph first. Other writers like to focus first on the body of the essay and write the introduction and conclusion later.

Rules to Remember

When writing a narrative essay, there are a few common rules to remember. Writing a narrative essay is one of the few times it is appropriate to write in the first person. When attempting to tell a compelling story that has happened to you, it is acceptable to use "I." In addition, an author writing a narrative essay may also write more emotionally or descriptively than is appropriate for other kinds of essays. Normally, when writing persuasive or cause-and-effect essays, authors strive for an objective, professional tone. But because narrative writing features stories, it is acceptable to open your writing to a unique and personal writing style.

When writing essays about controversial issues such as racism, it is important to remember that disputes over the material are common precisely because there are many different perspectives from which to evaluate your subjects. Remember to state your arguments in careful and measured terms. Evaluate your topic fairly—avoid overstating negative qualities of one perspective or understating positive qualities of another. Use examples, facts, and details to support any assertions you make.

The Narrative Essay

Narrative writing tells a story or describes an event. Stories are something most people are familiar with since childhood. When you describe what you did on your summer vacation, you are telling a story. Newspaper reporters write stories of daily news. Novelists write fictional stories about imagined events.

Essays often use stories as an attempt to persuade the reader. The previous section of this book provided you with examples of essays on racism. Most are persuasive essays that attempt to convince the reader to support specific arguments about issues regarding racism. In addition to making arguments, the authors of these essays also tell stories in which racism plays a part. They used narrative writing to do this.

Components of Narrative Writing

All stories contain basic components of *character, setting,* and *plot.* These components answer four basic questions—who, when, where, and what—that readers need to make sense of the story being told.

Characters answer the question of whom the story is about. In a personal narrative using the first-person perspective ("My family was the target of racism in our community"), the characters are the writer herself and whom she encounters. But writers can also tell the story of other people or characters ("The Thomas family was the target of racism in their community").

The *setting* answers the questions of when and where the story takes place. The more details given about characters and setting, the more the reader learns about them and the author's views toward them. Ted Gup's fourth paragraph in Viewpoint Five is a good example of vividly describing the setting in which his story takes place. He describes the murals and fliers that decorate the walls of Grandpa's Kitchen to place his reader in the offensive environment.

The *plot* answers the question of what happens to the characters. It often involves conflict or obstacles that a story's character confronts and must somehow resolve. An example: A man named Randy Johnson has to decide how to handle the racist behavior of a coworker. Should he confront the coworker? If so, how? Should he involve authorities? Similarly, Kevin J. Marinelli's plot in Viewpoint Six revolves around his struggle with the white supremacy movement and how he ended up on death row.

Some people distinguish narrative essays from stories by looking at essays as pieces of writing that have a point—a general observation, argument, or insight that the author wants to share with the reader. In other words, narrative essays also answer "why" questions: Why did these particular events happen to the character? Why is this story worth retelling? The story's point is the essay's thesis.

Using Narrative Writing in Persuasive Essays

Narrative writing can be used in persuasive essays in several different ways. Stories can be used in the introductory paragraph(s) to grab the reader's attention and to introduce the thesis. Stories can comprise all or part of the middle paragraphs that are used to support the thesis. They may even be used in concluding paragraphs as a way to restate and reinforce the essay's general point. Narrative essays may focus on one particular story or may draw upon multiple stories.

A story can also be used as one of several arguments or supporting points. Or a narrative can take up an entire essay. Some stories are so powerful that by the time the reader reaches the end of the narrative, the author's main point is clear.

In the following section you will read some model essays on racism that use narrative writing. You will also do exercises that will help you write your own narrative essays.

Racism in America

Editor's Notes As you read in Preface A in this section, narrative writing has several uses. In the real world, writers may incorporate the narrative technique into another type of essay, such as a persuasive essay or a compare-and-contrast essay. Instead of focusing their whole essay on a single story, they may use several different stories together. They may also choose to use narration only in portions of their essay.

The following essay uses pieces of narration to discuss how many Americans experience racism in their everyday lives. As you read this essay, pay attention to its components and how they are organized. Also note that all sources are cited using MLA style. For more information on how to cite your sources, see Appendix C. In addition, consider the following questions:

1. How does the introduction engage the reader's attention?
2. How is narration used in the essay?
3. What purpose do the essay's quotes serve?
4. Would the essay be as effective if it contained only general arguments, and the stories of John Baugh and Ted Gup were not included?

◻ Refers to thesis and topic sentences

◻ Refers to supporting details

Paragraph 1

Conceptions of race and ethnicity in the United States have changed dramatically in the last hundred years. At the dawn of the twentieth century, African Americans were treated as second-class citizens, and many public institutions, such as schools, buses, and movie theaters, were segregated. During World War II, Japanese Americans were rounded up, taken from their homes, and forced to live in camps where they were monitored. Other minorities rarely received justice in the American courts and were discriminated against when seeking jobs. Clearly, the United States at the start of the twenty-first century is a very different

How does the introduction ease into the essay's topic? Do you think it is effective?

nation. Officially it is a country of equal opportunity and equal education for people of all races, creeds, and religions. However, racism persists in quieter and less institutionalized ways than of eras past. Many Americans have painful and frustrating experiences with racism as they go about their everyday lives.

This is the essay's thesis statement. It clearly explains what will be explored.

Paragraph 2

Consider the story of John Baugh, an African American and a successful professor at Stanford University. When Baugh was looking for housing in a white community in Northern California, he experienced a subtle yet serious form of racism firsthand. His search for a home began encouragingly enough; he shortly had many appointments with landlords to view their properties. But once he met them in person and they realized he was black, the property owners dissuaded him from living in the white community by telling him there was nothing available for him (Kashef 35–36). To be turned away from housing because of one's race is not uncommon in other places in the United States. A study undertaken by the *Kansas City Star* in 1997, for example, found that white people who apply for mortgages are approved more often than black people who apply for mortgages (Sickenger). In the Kansas City area that year, lenders rejected high-income black applicants almost three times more often than white applicants with similar salaries. Moreover, black applicants were rejected nearly twice as often as whites who made less than they did. This subtle yet painful racism needlessly toughens the lives of hard-working African American families. It is unfair and wrong.

This paragraph introduces John Baugh and his experience looking for a house.

Citing evidence such as studies and statistics lends hard support to the anecdote of John Baugh.

Transitional phrases such as "moreover" keep the ideas in the essay moving.

These sentences conclude the paragraph's discussion.

Paragraph 3

Racism can be found in other types of American businesses, as journalist Ted Gup discovered in Cleveland, Ohio. Gup, who is Jewish, happened upon a restaurant called Grandpa's Kitchen, which is a deli owned by a Palestinian named Brahim "Abe" Ayad. In addition to being a restaurant owner, Ayad dislikes Jews. He has decorated his

The phrase "other types" transitions from the discussion of race-biased mortgages to the anti-Semitic restaurant.

restaurant with anti-Semitic images, including signs that accuse Jews of killing Jesus and murals that show Jews as monkeys wearing religious caps called yarmulkes. "The first thing I see as I pull up to the deli," writes Gup, "is the mural, a pastiche of offensive images and accusations. . . . Am I not now in hostile territory?" Indeed, anti-Semitism appears to be on the rise in the United States. A nationwide survey released in 2002 by the Anti-Defamation League (ADL), an organization that fights anti-Semitism, found that 17 percent of Americans—about 35 million people—hold negative or hostile views about Jews. This was up from 1998, when 12 percent of Americans held such views. The ADL has said that the survey reveals that "an undercurrent of Jewish hatred persists in America."

Well-placed quotes allow your characters to speak for themselves.

Quoting from authorities can lend your essay legitimacy.

Paragraph 4

The stories of John Baugh and Ted Gup are just two of countless painful events that Americans experience every day. Disappointingly, the advent of the Internet has made it even easier for people to spread their views or find others who already share them. Although many Americans may show no outward signs in their daily lives of being racist, once online they can view the Web sites of hate groups or reinforce their racist beliefs by communicating with others in chat rooms. In 2002 the Simon Wiesenthal Center, a human rights organization, counted at least three thousand neo-Nazi or otherwise hateful Web sites active on the Internet. In fact, every day more than five thousand people view the pages of Stormfront.org, what is believed to be the world's first hate Web site. The Internet is an especially powerful and dangerous medium for racists because it enhances the influence a single racist can have. As author Ros Davidson explains, "Not too many years ago, a single [Ku Klux] Klansman would have to go to a great deal of effort and spend quite a bit of money and find a sympathetic printer in order to produce a pamphlet that might reach 100 people. Now the same Klansman, for almost no money, is able to very quickly put up a Web site that has the potential to reach millions."

This is the topic sentence of the fourth paragraph. It previews what the paragraph will discuss.

These sentences develop the paragraph's thesis by exploring the topic in more depth.

Paragraph 5

Ted Gup said of his experience with Grandpa's Kitchen, "The [anti-Semitic] murals make me cringe, but I much prefer that [Abe's] feelings be out in the open. They tell me where I stand with Abe. They also invite the possibility, however slim, that we might find some sliver of common ground." Gup's willingness to reach out to someone who hates him for being a particular ethnicity is admirable considering the pain, humiliation, and frustration that racist encounters cause. Hopefully in the twenty-first century Americans will be able to eradicate the remaining currents of racism and truly achieve a just and equitable society for all citizens.

Ted Gup's words are used to transition from the previous material and present the topic of the concluding paragraph.

This sentence concludes the essay without restating its main point.

Works Cited

"Anti-Semitism on the Rise in America—ADL Survey on Anti-Semitic Attitudes Reveals 17 Percent of Americans Hold 'Hardcore' Beliefs." Anti-Defamation League, 11 June 2002 < http://www.adl.org/PresRele/ASUS_12/4109_12.htm > .

Davidson, Ros. "Web of Hate." *Salon* 16 Oct. 1998.

Gup, Ted. "At the Corner of Hate and Free Speech." *Washington Post* 5 Jan. 2003.

Kashef, Ziba. "This Person Doesn't Sound White." *ColorLines* Fall 2003.

Sickenger, Ted. "American Dream Denied: When the Door Is Locked to Buying a Home." *Kansas City Star* 28 Feb. 1999.

Exercise A: Create an Outline from an Existing Essay

It often helps to create an outline of the five-paragraph essay before you write it. The outline can help you organize the information, arguments, quotes, and evidence you have gathered in your research.

For this exercise, create an outline that could have been used to write the first model essay. This "reverse engineering" exercise is meant to help you become familiar with using outlines to classify and arrange information.

To do this you will need to

1. articulate the essay's thesis,

2. pinpoint important pieces of evidence,

3. flag quotes that supported the essay's ideas, and

4. identify key points that supported the argument.

Part of the outline has already been started to give you an idea of the assignment.

Outline

Write the essay's thesis:

I. Paragraph 2 topic: Daily racism experienced by African Americans

A. The story of John Baugh illustrates an example of racism experienced by African Americans

B. *Kansas City Star* investigation supports the Baugh narrative

II. Paragraph 3 topic:

A.

B. Rise of anti-Semitism around the country
   1. ADL quote supports the statistics

III. Paragraph 4 topic:

   A.

   B. The Internet increases the reach of hate-mongers
      1.

Write the essay's conclusion:

"Driving While Black" on the New Jersey Turnpike

Essay
Two

Editor's Notes The following narrative essay differs slightly from the first model essay. Although it is still a five-paragraph essay, its main point focuses on one story instead of using small pieces of several different stories. Also, instead of just one supporting paragraph, the story takes up most of the essay. This is just one model for writing a narrative essay.

The essay recounts the story of the 1998 New Jersey Turnpike shootings which focused the nation's attention on the problem of racial profiling. The characters, setting, and plot are recounted in more detail than they would be in a simple anecdote in order to better engage the reader in the story. In this way the author relies on the power of the story itself to make the essay's point that racial profiling is wrong.

The notes in the margins provide questions that will help you analyze how this essay is organized and written.

■ Refers to thesis and topic sentences

■ Refers to supporting details

Paragraph 1

In America it is illegal for police to detain a person unless they have a clear reason to believe that he or she is involved in criminal activity. But some law enforcement officers, using stereotypes that judge minorities to be more likely to commit crime than whites, engage in what is known as racial profiling to pick out potential criminals. Racial profiling encourages troopers to illegally target minorities and stop them for minor violations, then subject them to lengthy searches, abuse, or even arrest. This practice is so common that it has become known as "driving while black," a play on words to echo "driving while intoxicated." Attorney and legal professor David Harris considers racial profiling to be one of America's

What is the essay's thesis statement?

premier problems and has put the issue in the following way: "Skin color has become evidence of the propensity to commit crime, and police use this evidence against minority drivers on the road all the time." To appreciate how devastating racial profiling can be, consider the 1998 case of the New Jersey Turnpike shootings, a high-profile incident which brought nationwide attention to the issue.

Paragraph 2

This paragraph introduces us to the main characters of the story. It also establishes where the story takes place.

On April 23, 1998, four basketball players from New York—Rayshawn Brown, Leroy Grant, Danny Reyes, and Keshon Moore—were driving south on the New Jersey Turnpike. The four men, three black and one Latino, were on their way to North Carolina State University where they planned to try out for the school's basketball team. Around Exit 7A, however, two New Jersey state troopers, James Kenna and John Hogan, shone a spotlight into their van and pulled it over for speeding. The officers frequently pulled minority motorists over on this section of road, known to many law enforcement officials as "the drug corridor" because drug runners used it to traffic drugs between New York City and New Jersey.

Paragraph 3

This paragraph sets the plot in motion—the chronological actions and events that happen to the characters.

Seconds after the van was pulled over, however, the situation became more than just a routine traffic stop. The officers thought they saw the van back up toward them in a threatening way, so they fired eleven shots into the vehicle, hitting three of the four passengers. The athletes were seriously injured—later, they learned that the bullets were lodged in their bodies in such a way that it was dangerous to surgically remove them. After the men were shot at, they were handcuffed, strip-searched, and forced to lie in a ditch before paramedics were allowed to help them. However, instead of finding guns or drugs in the car, as the troopers thought they might, they found only a Bible in the backseat.

Paragraph 4

Nearly four years after the shootings, the state troopers publicly acknowledged in a court of law that they had stopped the athletes' vehicle only because they could see that its passengers were dark-skinned. The troopers admitted they had been trained to focus on minority drivers because their supervisors told them they were more likely to be drug traffickers. They also said they had intentionally lied about the race of drivers they had stopped in the past in order to conceal the fact that they were singling out blacks and Latinos. In the end, however, neither Kenna nor Hogan was sentenced to jail time or probation. They received just a $280 fine, although both men resigned from the state police and agreed to never serve in law enforcement again. Also, in February 2001 the New Jersey attorney general's office awarded the victims of the incident $12.9 million in damages. But outside of New Jersey, justice has not been achieved for the countless other victims of racial profiling.

> This paragraph describes the events, actions, and consequences that stem from the pivotal event.

Paragraph 5

The turnpike shootings came to symbolize the frustration of minority motorists all over the country who have for years complained that they are unfairly singled out by police solely because of their skin color. Indeed, data exists that show that minorities are stopped a disproportionately large number of times. In April 2001 the New Jersey attorney general released a report on traffic stop incidents that showed that over 75 percent of that state's two thousand traffic stops were of black or Latino drivers—yet according to the 2000 census, blacks and Latinos together make up only about 27 percent of New Jersey's population. Furthermore, only 19 percent of the stops resulted in arrests. The report also stated that officers are more likely influenced by stereotypes, which creates an atmosphere of discrimination among those

> What is the topic sentence of the last paragraph? How did you identify it?

The Lee quote is taken from the quote box in Viewpoint Four. Remember to retain information that you can quote to support your points.

who are supposed to protect and serve all Americans. Sadly, the story of an unjust traffic stop, and even one that ends in violence, comes as little shock to many Americans of color. This is why author Chisum Lee has declared, "the effort to end racial profiling [must be] part of the ongoing struggle to make the American dream of equality and dignity come true for everyone."

Works Cited

Harris, David. *Driving While Black: Racial Profiling on our Nation's Highways,* spec. report, ACLU, June 1999.

Lee, Chisum. "Civil Rights Rollback," *Village Voice* 3 Aug. 2004.

Exercise A: Identifying Components of the Narrative Essay

As you read in the section preface, narratives all contain certain elements, including *setting*, *character*, and *plot*. This exercise will help you identify these elements and place them in order in your paragraphs.

For this exercise you will isolate and identify the components of a narrative essay. Viewpoints Three and Five from Section One of this book are good sources to practice on. You may also, if you choose, use experiences from your own life or that of your friends.

Part A: Isolate and write down story elements.

Setting
The setting of a story is the time and place the main body of the story happens. Such information helps orient the reader. Does the story take place in the distant or recent past? Does it take place in a typical American community or an exotic locale?

Essay Two	Story taken from this volume	Story from personal experience
The New Jesey Turnpike Exit 7A April 23, 1998, 2001		

Character
Who is the story about? If there is more than one character, how are they related? At what stage of life are they? What are their aspirations and hopes? What makes them distinctive and interesting to the reader?

Essay Two	Story taken from this volume	Story from personal experience
Rayshaw Brown, Leroy Grant, Danny Reyes, Keshon Moore—four minority students who hope to play basketball on the university level. James Kenna, John Hogan—two white New Jersey State Troopers with a history of racial profiling.		

Pivotal Event

Most stories contain at least one single, discrete event on which the narrative hinges. It can be a turning point that changes lives or a specific time when a character confronts a challenge, comes to a flash of understanding, or resolves a conflict.

Essay Two	Story taken from this volume	Story from personal experience
The four basketball players are unjustly pulled over and shot at.		

Events/Actions Leading Up to the Pivotal Event

What are the events that happen to the characters? What are the actions the characters take? These elements are usually told in chronological order in a way that advances the action—that is, each event proceeds naturally and logically from the preceding one.

Essay Two	Story taken from this volume	Story from personal experience
Brown, Grant, Reyes, and Moore leave New York to try out for North Carolina State University's basketball team. They drive down the New Jersey Turnpike, traveling past the squad car of Kenna and Hogan.		

Events/Actions That Stem from Pivotal Event
What events/actions are the results of the pivotal event in the story? How were the lives of the characters of the stories changed?

Essay Two	Story taken from this volume	Story from personal experience
Three of the basketball players will have bullets lodged in them for the rest of their lives. They are awarded $12.9 million in damages. Kenna and Hogan lose their jobs as police officers and must pay a $280 fine.		

Point/Moral

What is the reason for telling the story? Stories generally have a lesson or purpose that is ultimately clear to the reader, whether the point is made explicitly or implied. Stories could serve as specific examples of a general social problem. They could be teaching tools describing behavior and actions that the reader should either avoid or emulate.

Essay Two	Story taken from this volume	Story from personal experience
The story illustrates the general presence and problems of racial profiling.		

Part B: Write down narrative elements in paragraph form.

Since stories vary greatly, there are many ways to approach telling them. One possible way of organizing the story elements you have structured is as follows:

Paragraph 1: Tell the reader the setting of the story and introduce the characters. Provide descriptive details of both.

Paragraph 2: Begin the plot—what happens in the story. Tell the events in chronological order, with each event advancing the action.

Paragraph 3: Describe the pivotal event in detail and its immediate aftermath.

Paragraph 4: Tell the short-term and/or long-term ramifications of the pivotal event. This paragraph could also include the point or moral of the story.

A Thanksgiving to Forget

Editor's Notes Essays drawn from memories or personal experiences are called personal narratives. The following essay is this type of narrative. It is not based on research or the retelling of someone else's experiences, such as the other narrative essays you have read in this book. Instead, this essay consists of an autobiographical story that recounts memories of an event that happened to the writer. The essay differs from the first two model essays in that it is written in the subjective or first-person ("I") point of view. It is also different in that it has more than five paragraphs. Many ideas require more than five paragraphs in order to be adequately developed. Moreover, the ability to write a sustained essay is a valuable skill. Learning how to develop a longer piece of writing gives you the tools you will need to advance academically. Indeed, many colleges, universities, and academic programs require candidates to submit a personal narrative as part of the application process.

As you read the following essay, take note of the sidebars in the margin. Pay attention to how it is organized and presented.

■ Refers to thesis and topic sentences

□ Refers to supporting details

Although racism is not the overt problem it was in the twentieth century, many Americans continue to hold racist beliefs and insist on stereotyping groups of people. I learned this lesson my freshman year in college, the way many painful lessons are learned: firsthand.

I will never forget how excited I was to get to campus and get settled in my dorm. Although some students dreaded the idea of dorm life, I always pictured it to be fun—like a never-ending slumber party, except without parents around to check up on you. On the first day of school, I met my roommates, Lindsey and Anna. I liked both of them

The opening sentence establishes the essay's topic.

immediately. We chatted as we set up our dorm room, and pretty soon we had the walls covered with band posters, pictures of movie stars, and tapestries. After I finished decorating my corner, I sat on my bed and viewed what the others were putting up. I noticed that Anna had hung both an American flag and a Mexican flag over her bed.

"A Mexican flag?" I asked. "Are you Mexican American?"

"*Si senorita!*" she said, with a laugh.

"This may sound weird," said Lindsey, "but you don't *look* Mexican."

"My family is very light-skinned," Anna explained. "In fact, I am often mistaken for a variety of races . . . white, Brazilian . . . someone even once thought I was Lebanese!" It was true—her curly, dark hair and pale skin did not identify her as any particular race.

As the semester progressed, Lindsey, Anna, and I became close friends. We studied together in the library and met in the café every Wednesday for lattes and a de-stress session. It seemed that we did something together every weekend. Being friends with Lindsey and Anna made the first semester of college breeze by, and before I knew it, classes were breaking for Thanksgiving.

Anna and I were both far from home and it was not possible for us to spend the holiday with our families. But when Lindsey heard that we were contemplating spending Thanksgiving in our dorm room with a couple of frozen turkey dinners, she quickly invited us to spend Thanksgiving with her family. Both of us agreed, thinking it would be fun to get off campus for a few days and see where Lindsey had grown up. Pretty soon we were on our first road trip together, on our way to Lindsey's house.

Lindsey's mom greeted us at the door. "Come in, come in!" she said. The house was warm and cozy, and the aroma of home-cooked food wafted out the door. I joined some of Lindsey's relatives in the living room while Anna offered to help Lindsey's mother in the kitchen.

I took a seat on the couch, in between Lindsey's Grandpa Will and her Aunt Betsy.

What do you learn about the characters in these sentences? What purpose does this material serve in the essay?

How does this paragraph serve to move the plot forward?

Note how using particular details helps the scene come to life.

"What is your major, dear?" asked Aunt Betsy.

"I'm studying political science," I said, and munched on some mixed nuts from a bowl on the coffee table.

"How interesting," she said. "Do you think one day you'll be a politician? Lord knows we could use some sensible leadership in this country!"

"Oh, don't get old Betsy started on politics," Lindsey's cousin Arthur said from across the room. "She'll talk your ear off about it all night!"

"Why Arthur," scolded Aunt Betsy, "I happen to know that you agree that our leaders are driving this country straight into the ground. Take immigration policy, for example. Or I should say, our *lack* of policy. At the current rate, all of us will soon be eating rice and beans while singing the national anthem in Spanish!"

My eyes widened—what was Aunt Betsy saying? I looked around, hoping that Anna had not heard Betsy's crude comment. She was talking with Lindsey's brother in the kitchen and seemed to be safely out of earshot. Suddenly I felt uncomfortable, and wondered if joining Lindsey's family for Thanksgiving would turn out to be a mistake. I was about to say something to Betsy about her stinging remark when Lindsey's mother called everyone to the table.

As the meal progressed, I slowly forgot about Betsy's comment and the group discussed other things. Like many families around the Thanksgiving table, conversation turned to food, football, and to events in the lives of family members who did not get to see each other as often as they would like. At one point, Lindsey's grandfather asked his son Larry, a teacher, how his classes were going this semester.

"Oh, you know—every year is the same," Larry replied. "Most of the kids are behaved, but there are always a couple of Pablos who frustrate the heck out of me."

I felt my blood run cold, and suddenly I knew the ugly conversation I had witnessed earlier in the living room had returned, and was about to get much worse.

"Do you know that some of these kids actually turn in papers to me half in English and half in Spanish?" continued

Does the dialogue sound natural to you? What details or features enhance it?

How is foreshadowing used in this paragraph? What purpose does it serve?

Larry. "I turn 'em right back and advise them to learn the language of this country that is generous enough to take care of them. I tell them, if they want to submit their paper in Spanish they can go to school back in Nogales or Tijuana or wherever their family crawled through the fence from. This is America, and we speak English here!"

My jaw dropped—I was appalled at such misguided, hurtful, ignorant remarks. Across the table, I saw Anna stiffen. Her brow crinkled as if she was trying to absorb what she just heard, trying to figure out if she should jump in or just let the horrible moment pass.

"Well Larry, aren't you just a saint for putting up with that," Aunt Betsy chimed in. "The Mexicans are all alike. They all come over here for a free ride. I mean, it is our tax dollars that pay for them to eat, that pay for them to have babies, and pay for those babies when they get sick. And the nerve of them to not even learn English! They're trying to Spanish-ize the schools just like they're trying to Spanish-ize the whole country."

"Spanish-ize? *Spanish-ize*?!" I blurted out, feeling as though I had to stop the conversation before it got worse. "Excuse me, but this conversation is making me uncomfortable. Not to mention that Anna is Mexican American!"

A hush fell over the table, and Anna looked at me as if she were in pain. Suddenly I realized that revealing her ethnicity might only make her feel more uncomfortable and awkward, like a sheep among wolves. I hadn't meant to "out" her in such a way—I had just been focused on my anger at what I was hearing.

Aunt Betsy was the first to speak. "Anna, dear, surely you can appreciate what we're saying. It's not that we dislike anyone per se, dear. It's just that as a group, Mexicans threaten the very character of this country. From changing the nature of our schools, to undercutting the wages of hardworking Americans . . . well, it's just very difficult to feel sympathy for such people. What does your mother do, hmmm dear? Does she clean houses? Maybe she doesn't charge as much as a professional service, cutting into their clientele? You can see what we mean, can't you dear? Surely you do."

"My mother," Anna said coolly, "is a real estate agent." With that, she stood up from the table, collected her purse, and went outside. Lindsey and I quickly followed her.

"Anna, I'm sorry about my family!" said Lindsey. "They tend to have . . . " she paused, "*ideas* about things."

"Ideas? *Ideas*?! Lindsey, they're racists!" yelled Anna. "How could you bring me into such an environment knowing your family held these crazy beliefs?"

"I'm sorry Anna, I didn't think it would come up," Lindsey said. "Also, I just thought . . . you know . . . you're *different* from the kind of people they're talking about. You're like, a *real* American, you're not a *border-jumper* or anything. . . ."

Anna sighed and shook her head. "I feel bad for you Lindsey. For you and your whole family."

She turned and began walking away. I could see her leafing around in her purse for her cell phone to call a cab.

"Anna, wait!" I yelled, but she put her hand up, indicating that she wanted to be alone.

I turned to Lindsey. "This is so embarrassing. Thanks for an unforgettable Thanksgiving," I said sarcastically.

The next day, Lindsey and I drove back to school, barely speaking to one another. When we got back to our dorm, we found that Anna had taken all of her things from our room. She had arranged with the dean of students to make an emergency transfer into another dorm. I tried on a number of occasions to get in touch with her, even if just to apologize for my role in the Thanksgiving debacle, but she seemed to not want to get into her feelings on the subject. Over time, we lost touch. Things were never the same between Lindsey and me, either. For the rest of the year we avoided each other, and each made friends with people whom we had more in common with. Pretty soon, the year was over, and we each went our separate ways. As the semesters rolled on I became absorbed with schoolwork and new friends. But I never forgot about Lindsey and Anna or the painful Thanksgiving that abruptly brought three promising friendships to a screeching halt.

> Note how the dialogue between Lindsey and Anna sounds natural and realistic. Can you picture them having this conversation?

> Note how the point of the essay is implicitly, rather than explicitly, made. Sometimes it is more powerful to let actions speak for themselves rather than trying to explain the obvious.

Exercise A: Practice Writing a Scene with Dialogue

The previous model essay used scene and dialogue to make a point. For this exercise, you will practice creative writing techniques to draft a one- or two-paragraph scene with dialogue. First, take another look at Essay Three and examine how dialogue is used.

When writing dialogue, it is important to:

1. Use natural-sounding language.
2. Include a few details showing character gestures and expressions as they speak.
3. Avoid overuse of speaker tags with modifiers, such as "he said stupidly," "she muttered softly," "I shouted angrily," and so on.
4. Indent and create a new paragraph when speakers change.
5. Place quotation marks at the beginning of and at the end of a character's speech. Do not enclose each sentence of a speech in quotation marks.

Scene-Writing Practice

Interview a classmate, friend, or family member. Focus on a specific question that pertains to racism, such as

- Have you ever been the victim of racism? What happened? What was it like?
- Have you ever made racist comments or told a racist joke? Why?
- Are you bothered by prejudice? Is anyone in your family prejudiced? How do you handle it?
- Why do you think people are racist?

Take notes while you interview your subject. Write down what he or she says as well as any details that are provided. Ask probing questions that reveal how the subject felt, what they said, and how they acted. Use your notes to create a brief one- or two-paragraph scene with dialogue.

But I Can't Write That

One aspect about personal narrative writing is that you are revealing to the reader something about yourself. Many people enjoy this part of writing. Others are not so sure about sharing their personal stories—especially if they reveal something embarrassing or something that could get them in trouble. In these cases, what are your options?

✔ Talk with your teacher about your concerns. Will this narrative be shared in class? Can the teacher pledge confidentiality?

✔ Change the story from being about yourself to a story about a friend. This will involve writing in the third person rather than the first person.

✔ Change a few identifying details and names to disguise characters and settings.

✔ Pick a different topic or thesis that you do not mind sharing.

Write Your Own Narrative Five-Paragraph Essay

Using the information from this book, write your own five-paragraph narrative essay that deals with racism. You can use the resources in this book for information about racism and how to structure a narrative essay.

The following steps are suggestions on how to get started.

Step One: Choose your topic.

The first step is to decide what topic to write your narrative essay on. Is there any subject that particularly fascinates you? Is there an issue you strongly support or feel strongly against? Is there a topic you feel personally connected to? Ask yourself such questions before selecting your essay topic. Refer to Appendix D: Sample Essay Topics if you need help selecting a topic.

Step Two: Write down questions and answers about the topic.

Before you begin writing, you will need to think carefully about what ideas your essay will contain. This is a process known as *brainstorming*. Brainstorming involves asking yourself questions and coming up with ideas to discuss in your essay. Possible questions that will help you with the brainstorming process include:

- Why is this topic important?
- Why should people be interested in this topic?
- How can I make this essay interesting to the reader?
- What question am I going to address in this paragraph or essay?
- What facts, ideas, or quotes can I use to support the answer to my question?

Questions especially for narrative essays include:

- Have I chosen a compelling story to examine?
- Does the story support my thesis statement?
- What qualities do my characters have? Are they interesting?

- Does my narrative essay have a clear beginning, middle, and end?
- Does my essay evoke a particular emotion or response from the reader?

Step Three: Gather facts, ideas, and anecdotes related to your topic.

This book contains several places to find information, including the viewpoints and the appendices. In addition, you may want to research the books, articles, and Web sites listed in Section Three or do additional research in your local library. You can also conduct interviews if you know someone who has a compelling story that would fit well in your essay.

Step Four: Develop a workable thesis statement.

Use what you have written down in Steps Two and Three to help you articulate the main point or argument you want to make in your essay. It should be expressed in a clear sentence and make an arguable or supportable point.

Examples:

Although the United States no longer formally practices segregation, many American communities continue to be divided along racial lines.

> (This could be the thesis statement of a narrative essay that examines the separation of race in America by looking at a few different communities in which blacks and whites live separately from each other.)

I had to face the uncomfortable truth that despite my best intentions, I harbored a certain sense of mistrust, dislike, and fear of people of particular races.

> (This could be the thesis statement of a narrative essay that uses the story of a woman who comes face to face with her racism to argue that Americans must become more self-aware.)

Step Five: Write an outline or diagram.

1. Write the thesis statement at the top of the outline.
2. Write roman numerals I, II, and III on the left side of the page with A, B, and C under each numeral.

3. Next to each roman numeral, write down the best ideas you came up with in Step Three. These should all directly relate to and support the thesis statement.
4. Next to each letter write down information that supports that particular idea.

Step Six: Write the three supporting paragraphs.

Use your outline to write the three supporting paragraphs. Write down the main idea of each paragraph in sentence form. Do the same thing for the supporting points of information. Each sentence should support the paragraph of the topic. Be sure you have relevant and interesting details, facts, and quotes. Use transitions when you move from idea to idea to keep the text fluid and smooth. Sometimes, although not always, paragraphs can include a concluding or summary sentence that restates the paragraph's argument.

Step Seven: Write the introduction and conclusion.

See Preface A for information on writing introductions and conclusions.

Step Eight: Read and rewrite.

As you read, check your essay for the following:

✔ Does the essay maintain a consistent tone?
✔ Do all paragraphs reinforce your general thesis?
✔ Do all paragraphs flow from one to the other? Do you need to add transition words or phrases?
✔ Have you quoted from reliable, authoritative, and interesting sources?
✔ Is there a sense of progression throughout the essay?
✔ Does the essay get bogged down in too much detail or irrelevant material?
✔ Does your introduction grab the reader's attention?
✔ Does your conclusion reflect back on any previously discussed material or give the essay a sense of closure?
✔ Are there any spelling or grammatical errors?

Section Three:
Supporting
Research
Material

Facts About Race in America

Editor's Note: These facts can be used in reports or papers to reinforce or add credibility when making important points or claims.

The Future of Race in America

The Census Bureau has made the following projections about the future of race in America:

- By the year 2035 there will be more than 50 million African Americans in the United States, making up 14.3 percent of the population.
- By the year 2040 there will be 87.5 million Hispanics in the United States, making up 22.3 percent of the population.
- By the year 2050 the Asian American population will grow to 37.6 million, making up 9.3 percent of the population.
- By the year 2060, white Americans will make up less than 50 percent of the total U.S. population.
- By the year 2100, white Americans will make up 40 percent of the total U.S. population.

Racial Disparity and Discrimination

- According to Focus Adolescent Services, more than one in four Hispanic students drop out of school. Nearly half leave school by the eighth grade.
- The Eisenhower Foundation calculates that of the 43 percent of children of color who attend public schools, more than half are poor. More than two-thirds fail to reach basic levels on national tests.
- The U.S. Census Bureau found that in 2003, the median U.S. household income for all races was $50,984; for

Asian households it was $60,803; white non-Hispanic households, $54,522; African American households, $38,354; and Hispanic households, $37,314.

- According to the American Civil Liberties Union (ACLU), African Americans and Hispanics in several different states were stopped for routine traffic violations in excess of their representation in the population.
- In Texas, African Americans and Hispanics were significantly more likely than whites to be searched following a traffic stop by Texas law enforcement agencies in 2004, according to the Texas Criminal Reform Commission.

According to the National Conference for Community and Justice (NCCJ),

- 64 percent of Americans believe racism is a problem in health care, 20 percent say it is a major problem;
- 60 percent of African Americans say that race or ethnic background affects getting routine medical care;
- in 2001 the U.S. Census Bureau reported that 10 percent of white Americans did not have health insurance compared to 19 percent of African Americans and 33.2 percent of Hispanics;
- heart disease mortality rates for adults ages twenty-five to sixty-four are almost twice as high among African Americans as whites;
- 68 percent of Americans believe racism is a problem in education, 20 percent say it is a major problem;
- 76 percent of Americans believe racism is a problem in the workplace, 23 percent say it is a major problem.

Race and Hatred

According to Tolerance.org, a Web project of the Southern Poverty Law Center,

- there are 762 active hate groups in the United States;
- there were at least 51 hate crimes reported in 2005;

- there were 221 hate crimes reported in 2004;
- there were nine reported cross-burnings in 2003 and eleven in 2004 in such places as Anderson, California, where a cross was burned in a black family's yard, and in Derby, Kansas, where a cross was burned on a Hispanic family's yard and a brick with a racial message written on it was thrown through one of the windows of their house;
- there were at least three hate rallies in 2005, the largest of which drew crowds of about 150 supporters, and there were eleven hate rallies in 2004, which each drew an average of about 32 supporters;
- the KKK operates 162 chapters in the United States.

    The ten states that have the most KKK chapters are
    1. Tennessee, 13 chapters;
    2. Ohio, 11 chapters;
    3. Texas, 10 chapters;
    4. North Carolina, 10 chapters;
    5. Arkansas, 10 chapters;
    6. Louisiana 9 chapters;
    7. Florida, 8 chapters;
    8. Georgia, 9 chapters;
    9. Alabama, 8 chapters;
    10. Kentucky, 7 chapters.

Finding and Using Sources of Information

No matter what type of essay you are writing, it is necessary to find information to support your point of view. You can use sources such as books, magazine articles, newspaper articles, and online articles.

Using Books and Articles

You can find books and articles in a library by using the library's computer or cataloging system. If you are not sure how to use these resources, ask a librarian to help you. You can also use a computer to find many magazine articles and other articles written specifically for the Internet.

You are likely to find a lot more information than you can possibly use in your essay, so your first task is to narrow it down to what is likely to be most usable. Look at book and article titles. Look at book chapter titles, and examine the book's index to see if it contains information on the specific topic you want to write about. (For example, if you want to write about racial profiling and you find a book about counterterrorism measures, check the chapter titles and index to be sure it contains information about racial profiling before you bother to check out the book.)

For a five-paragraph essay, you do not need a great deal of supporting information, so quickly try to narrow down your materials to a few good books and magazine or Internet articles. You do not need dozens. You might even find that one or two good books or articles contain all the information you need.

You probably do not have time to read an entire book, so find the chapters or sections that relate to your topic, and skim these. When you find useful information, copy it onto a notecard or into a notebook. You should look for supporting facts, statistics, quotations, and examples.

Using the Internet

When you select your supporting information, it is important that you evaluate its source. This is especially important with information you find on the Internet. Because nearly anyone can put information on the Internet, there is as much bad information as good information online. Before using Internet information—or any information—try to determine whether the source seems to be reliable. Is the author or Internet site sponsored by a legitimate organization? Is it from a government source? Does the author have any special knowledge or training relating to the topic you are looking up? Does the article give any indication of where its information comes from?

Using Your Supporting Information

When you use supporting information from a book, article, interview, or other source, there are three important things to remember:

1. *Make it clear whether you are using a direct quotation or a paraphrase.* If you copy information directly from your source, you are quoting it. You must put quotation marks around the information and tell where the information comes from. If you put the information in your own words, you are paraphrasing it.

Here is an example of a using a quotation:

Author Salim Muwakkil believes the American practice of using Native American symbols as team names should be put to rest. Writes Muwakkil: "The fight against Native American mascots and logos is a serious struggle to overturn the stereotypes and cultural assumptions that were forged in our racist past but still help determine the trajectories of our lives today" (9).

Here is an example of a brief paraphrase of the same passage:

Author Salim Muwakkil believes the American practice of using Native American symbols as team names should be put to rest. He argues that such names were given to team mascots and logos when racism was more acceptable in American culture. In the twenty-first century, however, he finds no place for such blatant racism, and calls on Americans to fight such stereotypes.

2. *Use the information fairly.* Be careful to use supporting information in the way the author intended it. There is a joke that movie ads containing critics' comments "First-Class!" and other glowing phrases take them from longer reviews that said something like, "This movie is first-class trash!" This is called taking information out of context. Using that information as supporting evidence is unfair.

3. *Give credit where credit is due.* Giving credit is known as citing. You must use citations when you use someone else's information, but not every piece of supporting information needs a citation.

   • If the supporting information is general knowledge—that is, it can be found in many sources—you do not have to cite your source.
   • If you directly quote a source, you must cite it.
   • If you paraphrase information from a specific source, you must cite it.

   If you do not use citations where you should, you are plagiarizing—or stealing—someone else's work.

Citing Your Sources

There are a number of ways to cite your sources. Your teacher will probably want you to do it in one of three ways:

   • Informal: As in the examples in number 1 above, you tell where you got the information in the same place you use it.

- Informal list: At the end of the article, place an unnumbered list of the sources you used. This tells the reader where, in general, you got your information.
- Formal: Use an endnote. An endnote is generally placed at the end of an article or essay, although it may be located in different places depending on your teacher's requirements.

Works Cited

Muwakkil, Salim. "Racist Slurs Taint U.S. Sports." *In These Times* 16 Feb. 2004.

Using MLA Style to Create a Works Cited List

You will probably need to create a list of works cited for your paper. These include materials that you quoted from, relied heavily on, or consulted to write your paper. There are several different ways to structure these references. The following examples are based on Modern Language Association (MLA) style, one of the major citation styles used by writers.

Book Entries

For most book entries you will need the author's name, the book's title, where it was published, what company published it, and the year it was published. This information is usually found on the inside of the book. Variations on book entries include the following:

A book by a single author:
> Guest, Emma. *Children of AIDS: Africa's Orphan Crisis*. London: Sterling, 2003.

Two or more books by the same author:
> Friedman, Thomas L. *From Beirut to Jerusalem*. New York: Double-day, 1989.
> ———. *The World Is Flat: A Brief History of the Twentieth Century*. New York: Farrar, Straus and Giroux, 2005.

A book by two or more authors:
> Pojman, Louis P., and Jeffrey Reiman. *The Death Penalty: For and Against*. Lanham, MD: Rowman & Littlefield, 1998.

A book with an editor:
> Friedman, Lauri S., ed. *At Issue: What Motivates Suicide Bombers?* San Diego, CA: Greenhaven, 2004.

Periodical and Newspaper Entries

Entries for sources found in periodicals and newspapers are cited a bit differently than books. For one, these sources usually have a title and a publication name. They also may have specific dates and page numbers. Unlike book entries, you do not need to list where newspapers or periodicals are published or what company publishes them.

An article from a periodical:
> Snow, Keith Harmon. "State Terror in Ethiopia." *Z Magazine* June 2004: 33–35.

An unsigned article from a periodical:
> "Broadcast Decency Rules." *Issues & Controversies On File* 30 Apr. 2004.

An article from a newspaper:
> Constantino, Rebecca. "Fostering Love, Respecting Race." *Los Angeles Times* 14 Dec. 2002: B17.

Internet Sources

To document a source you found online, try to provide as much information on it as possible, including the author's name, the title of the document, the date of publication or of last revision, the URL, and your date of access.

A Web source:
> Shyovitz, David. "The History and Development of Yiddish." Jewish Virtual Library 30 May 2005 < http://www.jewishvirtuallibrary.org/jsource/History/yiddish.html > .

Your teacher will tell you exactly how information should be cited in your essay. Generally, the very least information needed is the original author's name and the name of the article or other publication.

Be sure you know exactly what information your teacher requires before you start looking for your supporting information so that you know what information to include with your notes.

Sample Essay Topics

Race in American Society

Racism Is Declining in America

Racism Is Increasing in America

White Americans Are in Denial About Racism

White Americans Are Victims of Reverse Racism

Segregation Is a Thing of the Past

Social Segregation Still Exists

White Supremacists Pose a Serious Threat to Minorities

White Supremacists Do Not Pose a Serious Threat to Minorities

Minorities Will Soon Outnumber Whites in America

Intermarriages Display the Harmony of Americans

Intermarriages Expose the Racism of Americans

Being Politically Correct About Race Is Appropriate

Political Correctness Hampers Frank Conversation About Race in America

Racism in U.S. Policies and Institutions

Racism Is Institutionalized in America

Racism Is Not Institutionalized in America

The Death Penalty Is Racist

The Death Penalty Is Not Racist

Environmental Policies Are Racist

Environmental Policies Are Not Racist

The U.S. Government Should Pay Reparations to Blacks for Slavery

The U.S. Government Should Not Pay Reparations to Blacks for Slavery

Affirmative Action Helps Minorities

Affirmative Action Hurts Minorities

Affirmative Action Is Unfair to Hardworking Whites
Racial Profiling Is Unfair and Wrong
Racial Profiling Catches Criminals
Race-Based College Admissions Should Be
  Encouraged
Race-Based College Admissions Should Be Banned

Writing Prompts for Personal Narratives

Use another person's story or your own story to illustrate any of the topics listed above, or come up with a unique topic on your own. Describe what happened during an incident when you, a person you know, or someone you read about was in a situation that involved racism. Use research, interviews, or personal experience to tell the story so that it supports the point you want to make about racism.

Organizations to Contact

African Americans for Humanism (AAH)
PO Box 664, Buffalo, NY 14226 • (716) 636-7571
Web site: www.secularhumanism.org

AAH seeks to develop humanism in the secular African American community and fight racism through humanistic education.

American Civil Liberties Union (ACLU)
125 Broad St., 18th Floor, New York, NY 10004
(212) 549-2500 • Web site: www.aclu.org

The ACLU is a national organization that works to defend Americans' civil rights as guaranteed by the U.S. Constitution.

American Immigration Control Foundation (AICF)
PO Box 525, Monterey, VA 24465 • (703) 468-2022
The AICF educates the public on what its members believe are the disastrous effects of uncontrolled immigration.

Anti-Defamation League (ADL)
823 United Nations Plaza, New York, NY 10017
(212) 490-2525 • Web site: www.adl.org

ADL works to stop the defamation of Jews and to ensure fair treatment for all U.S. citizens.

Center for the Study of Popular Culture (CSPC)
9911 W. Pico Blvd., Suite 1290, Los Angeles, CA 90035
(310) 843-3699 • Web site: www.cspc.org

CSPC is a conservative educational organization that addresses topics such as political correctness, cultural diversity, and discrimination. Its civil rights project promotes equal opportunity for all individuals and provides legal assistance to citizens challenging affirmative action.

Citizens' Commission on Civil Rights (CCCR)

2000 M St. NW, Suite 400, Washington, DC 20036
(202) 659-5565 • e-mail: citizens@cccr.org
Web site: www.cccr.org

CCCR monitors the federal government's enforcement of antidiscrimination laws. It publishes reports on affirmative action and desegregation.

Hispanic Policy Development Project (HPDP)

1001 Connecticut Ave. NW, Suite 901, Washington, DC 20036
(202) 822-8414

HPDP encourages the analysis of public policies affecting Hispanics in the United States, particularly the education, training, and employment of Hispanic youth.

National Association for the Advancement of Colored People (NAACP)

4805 Mt. Hope Dr., Baltimore, MD 21215-3297
(410) 358-8900

The NAACP is the oldest and largest civil rights organization in the United States. Its principal objective is to ensure the political, educational, social, and economic equality of minorities.

National Urban League

120 Wall St., 8th Floor, New York, NY 10005
(212) 558-5300 • Web site: www.nul.org

A community service agency, the National Urban League's stated aim is to eliminate institutional racism in the United States. It also provides services for minorities who experience discrimination in employment, housing, welfare, and other areas.

Poverty and Race Research Action Council (PRRAC)

3000 Connecticut Ave. NW, Suite 200, Washington, DC 20008
(202) 387-9887 • e-mail: info@prrac.org

The Poverty and Race Research Action Council is a non-partisan, national, not-for-profit organization convened by major civil rights, civil liberties, and antipoverty groups. PRRAC's purpose is to link social science research to advocacy work in order to successfully address problems at the intersection of race and poverty.

The Prejudice Institute
Stephens Hall Annex, TSU, Towson, MD 21204-7097
(410) 830-2435

The Prejudice Institute is a national research center concerned with violence and intimidation motivated by prejudice. It conducts research, supplies information on model programs and legislation, and provides education and training to combat prejudicial violence.

United States Commission on Civil Rights
624 Ninth St. NW, Suite 500, Washington, DC 20425
(202) 376-7533

A fact-finding body, the commission reports directly to Congress and the president on the effectiveness of equal opportunity laws and programs.

Bibliography

Books

Cashin, Sheryll, *The Failures of Integration: How Race and Class Are Undermining the American Dream*. New York: Public Affairs, 2004.

Corlett, J. Angelo, *Race, Racism, and Reparations*. Ithaca, NY: Cornell University Press, 2003.

Graves, Joseph L., Jr., *The Race Myth: Why We Pretend Race Exists in America*. New York: Oxford University Press, 2004.

Hanson, Victor Davis, *Mexifornia: A State of Becoming*. New York: Encounter Books, 2003.

Kennedy, Randall, *Nigger: The Strange Career of a Troublesome Word*. New York: Pantheon Books, 2002.

Kete, Molefi, *Erasing Racism: The Survival of the American Nation*. Amherst, NY: Prometheus Books, 2003.

Loonin, Meryl, *Overview: Multicultural America*. San Diego: Lucent Books, 2004.

MacDonald, Heather, *Are Cops Racist?* Chicago: Ivan R. Dee, 2003.

Mathis, Deborah, *Yet a Stranger: Why Black Americans Still Don't Feel at Home*. New York: Warner Books, 2002.

Meeks, Kenneth, *Driving While Black: What to Do If You Are a Victim of Racial Profiling*. New York: Broadway Books, 2000.

Pincus, Fred, *Reverse Discrimination: Dismantling the Myth*. Boulder, CO: Lynne Rienner, 2003.

Swain, Carol M., *The New White Nationalism in America: Its Challenge to Integration*. Cambridge, England: Cambridge University Press, 2002.

Wood, Peter, *Diversity: The Invention of a Concept*. New York: Encounter Books, 2003.

Wynter, Leon E., *American Skin: Pop Culture, Big Business, and the End of White America.* New York: Crown, 2002.

Periodicals

Burgess, Julia, "Healthy Homes," *Poverty & Race,* July/August 2004.

Chavez, Linda, "NAACP Leaders Are Stuck in a Time Warp," *Conservative Chronicle,* July 16, 2003.

Fein, Bruce, "Tackling a Root Cause of Terrorism," *Washington Times,* December 21, 2004.

Fitzpatrick, James K., "The Racial Profiling Hustle," *Wanderer,* May 30, 2002.

Fuller, Howard, "The Struggle Continues," *Education Next,* Fall 2004.

Golab, Jan, "How Racial P.C. Corrupted the LAPD (and Possibly Your Local Force as Well)," *American Enterprise,* June 2005.

Greenblatt, Alan, "Race in America," *CQ Researcher,* July 11, 2003.

Hume, Mick, "What's Wrong with a Little Hate?" *The Times* (London), July 12, 2004.

Keating, Martha H., and Felicia Davis, "Air of Injustice," *Christian Social Action,* January/February 2003.

Johnson, Kirk, "New Tactics, Tools, and Goals Are Emerging for White Power Organizations," *New York Times,* April 6, 2005.

MacDonald, Heather, "What Looks Like Profiling Might Just Be Good Policing," *Los Angeles Times,* January 19, 2003.

Malkin, Michelle, "Jacko and Snoop Dogg's America," *Conservative Chronicle,* February 9, 2005.

McWhorter, John H., "As Racism Recedes, More Blacks Shift to Political Center," *Los Angeles Times,* March 17, 2004.

Muwakkil, Salim, "Racist Slurs Taint U.S. Sports," *In These Times,* January 21, 2004.

Taylor, Keeanga-Yamahtta, "Racism in America Today," *International Socialist Review,* November/December 2003.

Yost, Mark, "A Team Named Sioux," *Wall Street Journal,* December 27, 2002.

Web Sites

Center for Democracy and Technology (www.cdt.org). The Center for Democracy and Technology is concerned with constitutional liberties in the digital age. It seeks practical solutions to enhance free expression and privacy in global communications technologies.

Department of Homeland Security (www.dhs.gov). Offers a wide variety of information on homeland security, including press releases, speeches and testimony, and reports on new initiatives in the war on terrorism.

National Immigration Forum (NIF) (www.immigration forum.org). Advocates public policies that welcome immigrants and refugees and that are fair and supportive to newcomers to the United States. The NIF Web site offers a special section on immigration in the wake of September 11.

Patriots to Restore Checks and Balances (www.checks balances.org). An anti–Patriot Act group comprised of individuals who believe the act infringes on the rights of law-abiding Americans.

Preserving Life & Liberty (www.lifeandliberty.gov). Set up by the U.S. Department of Justice to address civil libertarians' concerns about the Patriot Act and other homeland security initiatives. Offers answers to frequently asked questions about the Patriot Act and testimony from U.S. officials in support of the act.

Index

Picture Credits

Cover: © Paul McErlane/Reuters/CORBIS
AP/Wide World Photos, 41, 43
© Bettmann/CORBIS, 12
© CORBIS, 37 (inset)
Bob Daemmerich/AFP/Getty Images, 37
© Najlah Feanny/SABA/CORBIS, 25
© Ed Kashi/CORBIS, 13
Vincent Kessler/Reuters/Landov, 41 (inset)
Harold M. Lambert/Hulton Archive/Getty Images, 45
© Robin Nelson/Photo Edit, 49
Sue Ogrocki/Reuters/Landov, 21
© Reuters/CORBIS, 30 (inset)
Mario Tama/Getty Images, 14
© Peter Turnley/CORBIS, 30
Victor Habbick Visions, 19, 35, 51

About the Editor

Lauri S. Friedman earned her bachelor's degree in religion and political science from Vassar College. Much of her studies there focused on political Islam, and she produced a thesis on the Islamic Revolution in Iran titled *Neither West, Nor East, But Islam.* She also holds a preparatory degree in flute performance from the Manhattan School of Music, and is pursuing a master's degree in history at San Diego State University. She has edited over ten books for Greenhaven Press, including *At Issue: What Motivates Suicide Bombers?, At Issue: How Should the United States Treat Prisoners in the War on Terror?* and *Introducing Issues with Opposing Viewpoints: Terrorism.* She currently lives near the beach in San Diego with her yellow lab, Trucker.